NEW YORK TIMES & USA TODAY BESTSELLING AUTHOR

NICOLE BLANCHARD

ANCHOR

A FIRST TO FIGHT NOVEL

Anchor

Copyright © 2016 by Nicole Blanchard

Bolero Books LLC
11956 Bernardo Plaza Dr. #510
San Diego, CA 92128
www.buybolerobooks.com

DEDICATION

To Bruce Willis and Keanu Reeves

CONTENTS

CHAPTER ONE

GABRIEL

I wish I could say it was the sexy blonde who'd been wrapped around me like ivy on a pole all night who woke me, but it isn't her sugar-sweet voice blaring through my cellphone speaker.

"I swear to God, Gabriel, if you aren't there at six o'clock on the dot to pick up Emily, I'm going to the lawyers to renegotiate custody."

"Don't threaten me, Taylor," I say with a weariness now characteristic of all our conversations. What I wish I could do is bark orders at her. It'd be so much easier if I could deal with my ex-wife like I do the men under my command. It would have made being married to her a hell of a lot more bearable. Pulling on a pair of pants and choking down a swallow of coffee from a forgotten mug on my nightstand distracts me long enough so I don't go off on her ass. "It's not even seven in the morning. I know what time I have to be there."

Behind me, the blonde stretches on the white cotton sheets, and I take a moment to admire the miles of tanned skin before I duck out the sliding glass doors leading from my bedroom to my back patio. My dog Rudy is hot on my heels and streaks across the pavers to water the bushes and dive in the pool with a gorgeous view of the beach.

She snorts, and I have to wonder what possessed me to marry her. "That's what you said the last time, and I waited by the ferry for over an hour. This is why we got divorced. You never do what you say you will."

"I told you, I had an emergency. You know I volunteer with the Coast Guard. Search-and-rescue missions don't just fit into a schedule." I keep my voice calm and level, but when Taylor's pissed, she's like a spooked Chihuahua—she can't seem to stop yapping.

"Yeah," she says in a tone I have heard way too often over the years, clipped with a dash of bitter. It's about as appetizing as the two-day old coffee I'm drinking. "You can be there for everyone but your family, right? You've got a lot of lives to save, but you keep missing the ones right in front of you."

I sigh into the phone. It's too early for this shit.

Taylor gives a half laugh, devoid of humor. "Right. We'll see you tonight at six o'clock." There's a pause, and I know she wants me to fill it with apologies and assurances, but I'm done with apologizing to her. As soon as the ink was dry on our divorce papers, I didn't look back. "Don't be late, Gabe. Okay?"

There's static, some background chatter, and then a bright, bubbly voice comes over the line. One that melts the frown right off my face and makes the day seem brighter, even on this side of noon. "Daddy? Hi, Daddy!"

"Hey there, sugar plum." My voice warms and the tension eases from my shoulders.

"Whatcha doing?" Emily laughs, causing me to smile.

"Watching Rudy swim." Rudy lurches from the pool to bring me a ball, and I throw it back in the water for him. "What are you doing? Can't wait to see you tonight."

"Can't wait to see you, Daddy," she says and then describes her summer school, her friends, and any other thought traipsing across her five-year-old brain in vivid detail. I could listen to her talk for hours. She's about the only female I can stand for any length of time.

As she chatters on, I amble across the sand-colored, concrete pavers and sit down next to the pool, my cup of coffee by my side. Rudy paddles over with the neon yellow tennis ball clamped between his jaws. I wrestle it from him and then throw the ball to the far side of the pool. He splashes in, ignorant of all of my human problems, and dog-paddles to his goal.

The sound of the sliding glass door draws my eyes back to the house, and I find the blonde posed in the doorway. The white sheet is draped around her body and offers teasing glimpses of her toned legs and ass. And she is toned. Everywhere. I spent many, many hours getting well acquainted with every part of her last night.

Her smile is seductive and would have any man on his knees begging for round two, but verbal sparring with Taylor left a bad taste in my mouth. As she sashays across the lawn, my sole concern is for the very expensive Egyptian cotton sheet she's getting grass-stained.

Maybe I'm losing my touch. Six or seven years ago, it took only the slightest glance at a half-dressed woman to get me in the mood.

Now it almost seems like a production just to get off.

Emily wraps up her updates, and I refocus on our conversation. "I can't wait for you to tell me all about the rest when you get here. Don't forget Mr. Wolfie, okay? We'll take him for a ride around the island."

As if she could forget him. She clings to the stuffed wolf I gave her before my last deployment as if she'd die without it.

She told me once it smells like me, and when she has it with her, it's almost like I'm with her, too.

Kids have a way of sucker punching you in the heart.

It wasn't long after her admission that I decided to stick closer to home and retired from my long career with the Marines. I never thought I'd give that up for anything, but when there's a two-foot-nothing, bleach-blonde little angel crying because you're never home, your priorities change. It becomes about them instead of you.

I hope I didn't realize it too late.

Volunteering with the Coast Guard seemed like the

perfect balance between my need to serve my community and country and my desire to be closer to my daughter. Once I decided to leave the Marines, I moved back to Rockaway Island where I grew up and took over my dad's tourist boating business. Weekends like this, when I know it'll be hours instead of months until I see her again, make those sacrifices worth it.

"Okay, Daddy." Her giggle fills my ears. "Loves you!"

I glance back at the blonde as Emily sends me her love. Maybe the reason I can't commit to another woman isn't because I'm not interested. Maybe it's because I don't want to disappoint the most important one in my life—my daughter. "Loves you, too, sweetheart."

I hang up, and a small hand pulls me to my feet. The blonde reaches down and draws me against her. My fingers linger on her hips, but then they move to her arms, my touch causing her to shiver. She mirrors my movements and wraps her arms around me. There's a slight pause where I'm tempted to take her back to bed, but the temptation is not enough to rip the blanket off her and get reacquainted.

"Thanks for a great time," she says. Her voice is still hoarse from all the screaming she did. The cottage I inherited from my parents after they died is a good mile from any neighbor, which is a good thing. If it were closer, we would have kept them up half the night. I feel bad about turning her away. Almost.

I kiss her, taking care not to be too rough on her swollen lips. Because I enjoy the kiss, I lengthen it until her nails dig into my skin. I'm not an asshole, and I don't use women, but I make sure they enjoy our time together. My dad taught me that much before I left at eighteen to explore parts unknown and take down bad guys. The women I spend time with know up front our relationships won't go any deeper than twisting the sheets.

"Same time tomorrow?" she asks as she pulls away, gasping softly to catch her breath. Her chin is tipped up to face me, and she bites her lip as she waits for my response.

"Sorry, can't. I'll be busy." I trail a finger down her arm and enjoy how she shivers against me. "But this was fun."

"It was." Her eyes flick down to my lips, and I have to hold back my own smile. "See you later?"

I take a step away as though to help her back up the steps, but really I'm just ready for her to leave. "Maybe."

I give her a final kiss, and she walks back into the house to get dressed as I walk back to my previous spot by the pool. A little while later, I hear the front door open and close and then a car starts and drives down the gravel driveway.

Rudy paddles up to me, and I throw the ball back to him a couple of times. I check the forecast on my phone for the afternoon and note a squall spinning up west of the island. It shouldn't take a turn in our direction, but I make a note to keep an eye on it.

Even so, I'll keep my ringer on and my phone clipped to my belt for the rest of the day.

If I've learned anything from my years marching through deserts, hacking through jungles, and weathering waves the size of skyscrapers, it's luck can change in an instant. In my experience, when everything is going well, things always take a turn for the worse.

CHLOE

"It'll be fun!" my boss says. Her hands lift in a conciliatory gesture when I blow my bangs out of my face and frown. "Well, okay, maybe not, but there will be beaches and lots of sun. Maybe you'll even get a tan!"

I throw my head back against my desk chair and stare up at a familiar patch of ceiling. "I don't need a tan, Sienna. What I need is a vacation."

"Does it count if the business trip is to a popular vacation spot? Vacation by association?" Her voice tilts up at the end, and I can't fault her for trying to make the best of a bad situation.

"Why do you have to move again?" I ask, refraining from banging my head on the desk in frustration.

She smiles, but it wobbles around the edges. "You know you're the best, right Chloe?"

"Sure, I am." I glance with repressed yearning I hope she can't see at the calendar on my desk with this weekend circled with hearts. I'd planned to veg out on the couch with a marathon of romantic movies and no phone, laptop or work-related web time, but I'll just have to suck it up. "You so better love me for this."

"I do, you know I do." She rounds my desk and envelopes me in a hug. "You aren't my best friend for nothing!"

"Just promise you'll write whenever you get where you're going. If your plans don't pan out, you can call me. Whatever you need, I'm there."

"I would say you should hook up with someone when you get to the island, but we both know it won't happen."

"Speaking of," I say, and she groans. Papers rustle and flutter to the floor as I sort through the organized chaos on my desk. "What will I be doing at," I squint at the fine print, "Rockaway Island?"

"The usual. It's a potential investment opportunity for one of our clients. They're interested in turning it into an upscale bed-and-breakfast. If they book through us, we get a twenty-five percent commission. You'll need to take a look at the property, get pictures. Work your magic."

"You owe me." I'm the one who owes her. If it weren't for Sienna, I'd probably be homeless.

When I graduated from college, I expected to move in with my boyfriend. When I moved all the way to Jacksonville, he informed me he'd had a change of heart. He'd realized he couldn't compromise our friendship by marrying me. Once I got over the betrayal and shock, I realized I needed a place to live and a job to support myself as soon as possible. I couldn't look at him, let alone stay in the same apartment we'd planned to live in together.

I'd met her through an employment agency and she not only gave me a position as a receptionist at her boutique travel agency, but also let me crash at her place until I could afford to save up for my own.

Whenever she needs a favor, I'm there. No matter what it is.

"Promise," she says. "Anything you need."

"I'll hold you to that."

———

I was going to be late.

I hated to be late.

As a rule, I arrived at scheduled places ten minutes prior to being ten minutes early. My father always said, "If you're on time, you're late."

Well, according to his philosophy, I was *very, very* late.

"Shit, shit, shit," I hiss, as I whirl like a dervish around my apartment, tossing clothes pell-mell into suitcases. Most of them tumble to the floor in a heap guaranteed to cause me endless irritation when I get home and see it, but I don't have time to obsess about the disorganized mess.

The ferry scheduled to transport tourist down the St. John's River and then fifteen miles off the east coast to Rockaway Island is scheduled to leave in half an hour.

With a frustrated curse, I scrub my hands through my hair and glance around my apartment for anything I may have left behind. My eyes skip over random stacks of my belongings, not taking anything in. I have to force myself to slow my breathing to focus.

Camera. *Check.*

Chargers. *Check.*

Extra SD cards. *Check.*

Phone, cash, suitcase. *Check, check and check.*

The essentials are tucked into Ziploc bags and then into their respective cases. I'm a natural klutz, and when given the opportunity, have ruined any electronic gadget in the vicinity. During college, I murdered countless phones, multiple laptops, and more cords, chargers, and small appliances than I can count. I take extra care with any work-related tech. It's become a running joke at work and I don't need to see the look on Sienna's face if I ruin yet another phone or tablet.

As I walk out the door with my camera case slung over my shoulder and suitcase in hand, I shoot off a quick text to my neighbor to feed my goldfish while I'm gone. Those, I haven't killed. Yet.

This is why I don't see my ex standing outside my door and run right into him.

See? Klutz.

"Jesus, Chloe," he says and, like he had a million times while we were together, he throws up his arms to steady me. "What's the rush?"

My heart, the traitorous thing, hammers in my chest and I hope it's from being startled rather than from the man himself. "I'm late for a work thing."

I re-shoulder my camera bag and study him. He's too handsome, with dark blonde hair, a firm jaw and straight nose.

All-American. Clean cut. The man I always pictured I'd be with.

Thomas rocks back on his heels. "You look good."

Nodding is the only response I can seem to come up with and when I realize how foolish I must look, I clear my throat. "Um, thanks. Look, I really—"

When I try to maneuver around him, he blocks my path. "I wanted to talk to you. It'll just take a second."

He has his hands in his jeans pockets and I know it means he's feeling extra vulnerable. I have to clench my hands around my suitcase handle to keep from comforting him. *Comforting him!* He shouldn't get to be vulnerable. He shouldn't get to be the damaged one in this scenario. I was the one who lost everything. I lost my best friend and my fiancé all in one go.

If anyone deserves to be pissed or comforted, it's me.

But I know it'll be faster for me to just listen to what he has to say. Arguing will cost me precious minutes, and the clock is ticking. "What is it?"

"I don't know how to say this, except for me to just come out with it."

Now I'm wishing I had just walked right by him. My fingers clutch around the handle to my suitcase and I take an extra breath to stem any emotional reaction at all.

"I'm getting married." He whispers it, like if he's gentle enough, the words won't feel like bullets aimed straight at my heart.

My grip on the suitcase keeps me from stumbling backward. "I—," I clear my throat and then try again. "That's great, Thomas. Wonderful. Congratulations."

He leans forward like he wants to comfort me and I find myself taking an automatic step in retreat. His lips part in shock, then he checks himself, schooling his features.

I'd always been a demonstrative girlfriend, and then fiancé, and I'm not ashamed to admit it. I doled out affection without a thought as to keeping it all to myself. Thomas was always a guy who never got enough and took everything I had to give without much in return. My mouth drops open and I shake my head.

I can't believe it took me learning about his impending nuptials to realize I deserve so much better.

"Is there anything else?" I ask when he doesn't say anything.

He frowns. "No, that's it. I didn't want you to hear it from someone else."

"Yeah, I appreciate it," I say and then I start forward. "I really do need to go before I'm late."

When he doesn't make a move to get out of my way, I roll my suitcase right around him.

I don't bother saying goodbye, I don't even turn and look back. I learned my lesson and it's not one I will forget: love and relationships are overrated. When I'm in the car, I focus on navigating traffic and checking the clock. Thomas and that part of my life are history and I'm putting them behind me.

According to the schedule Sienna printed out for me, I have ten minutes to make it to the ferry before it takes off and it's the last one scheduled to go out before the long holiday weekend. The docks are packed with people. Families heading to the island for summer vacation, co-eds for the parties, and businessmen for exclusive retreats. I navigate through the crowd with practiced ease and make it to the on-boarding area with minutes to spare.

It's a beautiful day and as I wait for the attendant to take my money and hand me change, I lift my face into the sea breeze, determined to enjoy the moment and put the past where it belongs—behind me. I take the change and roll my things to the gate where a crowd of people wait to walk up the ramp to the ferry. They haven't started boarding, so I'm in luck.

While I wait, I give myself a few minutes of time to think about Thomas and his confession. I'm pleased to find I don't feel like breaking down into a sobbing mess. If anything, a weight has been lifted off my shoulders and for the first time in a long time, there's a bounce in my step.

As people in front of me move forward, I smile at a little girl holding a stuffed wolf who is in line in front of me and she smiles back, showing two missing front teeth. Her mother stands next to her, frowning into her cell phone.

She's just redialing a number when a man bumps into her. The mother glances over and apologizes, but the man doesn't seem to pay her much mind. In fact, he walks with grim deter-mination to the boarding ramp, skipping everyone in line.

I step out of the line to express my indignation at his rude-ness when he turns and I realize he's holding a gun.

CHAPTER TWO

GABRIEL

THE BOATING SAFETY class I teach runs long. In part because
the students are curious, but the real reason is because I love
being on the water. It's what inspired me to join the Marines
after high school and what cemented my decision to volunteer
for the Coast Guard when I got out. And I'll admit to myself,
though I'd never say it aloud, I kinda enjoy the teaching
aspect, too. Something I never got to do in the Marines.
Badasses don't like being told when they're doing something
wrong.

"If you have questions," I say when the chatter has died
down, "please don't hesitate to give me a call and stay safe out
there."

I leave before anyone can bring up the search and rescue
missions, which seem to be a hot topic among the safety courses. Most of the instructors don't mind chatting about it after-

ward, but makes my skin crawl. I scrub a hand over my face as I walk down the hall to the exit. Whispers follow behind me and I don't have to guess what they're talking about.

It was easier when there was an enemy to face. When the bad guys were bad *guys*. People. Living, breathing things I could combat with weapons.

A mission is so much easier to complete when the bad guys stay down after a shot to the head or the heart. Combatting an enemy with no end, no conscience, and even less regard for human life than any degenerate I've ever come across is infinitely harder.

The elements don't have compassion. The ocean doesn't give a rat's ass about the lives it takes.

It's unforgiving. Relentless. Never-ending. Unconquerable.

And I both love and hate it.

Until a few months ago, I enjoyed battling the unpredictability, pitting my will against it. It is the ultimate rush.

Until I realized I could never stand a chance against Mother Nature.

The shack on the beach, where I run the part-time tourist business that pays the bills, offers little reprieve from the late summer sun. Its neon colors have long since faded from the combination of wind, salt, and water to ghosts of their former selves, the wood worn smooth by the constant breeze from the water. A lone figure rests against the counter flirting up a pretty customer.

My mood lifts when I recognize the old man, his

customary bottle of Coke, and his lazy smile. "Don't let him lie to you," I say to the girl. "He doesn't even work here."

Tyler snorts. "I'm here more than you are, I might as well work here. Here are your keys, darlin', the rental lasts through the day. Key return is at five on the dot."

She smiles at him and flounces off with two of her giggling girlfriends.

"Official business?" I say and nod to his police uniform. He and my dad were on the local force—which isn't saying much since the edges of the island are within spitting distance of each other. He's more like an uncle and has made it a point to keep tabs on me ever since my parents died in a freak boating accident a couple years ago.

"Sure," he says as he pops open a soda from the mini fridge I keep below the counter. "Ready to spread 'em?"

A plane buzzes over our heads, but I dismiss it as another advertisement or parasailing operation running in loops across the beach. Gulls caw in the distance and circle around forgotten snacks for their lunch. A car beeps, but it sounds far away. Above all is the constant rush of waves smashing into the surf. It was a sound that used to haunt me, but one I can't quite escape on the island.

Tyler offers a soda, and I drink it in a few gulps. "You're living the dream, man," he says as he sips his own. "Come and go as you please, a new hot woman every night. Fuck, I hate you."

A list of the day's activities sits on the counter and I shoot him a disbelieving look as I glance over it. "I doubt you'll be in possession of your balls tomorrow if your wife ever hears you say something like that."

Tyler winces. "You're probably right." He smiles, his otherwise hard eyes going soft. "God bless her."

Paperwork is the least favorite of my many responsibilities, so I always save it for last. Tyler likes to come at the end of his shift to keep one eye on the beach bunnies while the other watches his back. His wife, Selena, is a sweet lady, but she has a mean side. They've been happily married for twenty years and it's sort of a running joke on the island that he has a wandering, but harmless, eye. As long as I've known him, he's loved Selena to tears.

It's the relationship I always thought I wanted. Unfortunately, marriage turned out to be a whole other beast altogether. One I'm more than relieved to stay away from.

We bullshit for the next hour until my phone bleats out a familiar ringtone. Tyler gets a call on his radio at the same time.

The squall didn't listen to the forecasts because it's headed right for us—from the Atlantic side—and a couple of vacationers are trapped in the vicious waves.

A familiar rush of fear and excitement washes over me.

"Guess we're closing early," I say to Tyler.

———

A few hours later, I stumble back to my house for a shave and a change of clothes. I'm cutting it close, too close, to my pick up time for Emily. The small boat caught way too far off the coast due to the weather, took a lot more time to locate than we'd expected due to signal interruptions and a damn uncooperative tropical storm. We found the tourists healthy and uninjured. The storm blew itself out, leaving a sunny evening for Emily's ride over to the island on the ferry.

But I don't think Taylor will care about the weather or the lives we saved.

She won't hear anything from my explanation other than the "I'm late." My hope is she's joking about taking me back to court about custody.

Somehow I don't think it was an empty threat.

Another helicopter roars overhead, but I pay it no mind as I hurry to let Rudy piss before shutting him up in his cage until Em and I get back. By the time I get him fed and watered and left whining in the bathroom, my phone has rung multiple times.

I can already imagine Taylor's high-pitched voice screeching over the line, so I'm not in any rush to answer it and by the time I'm in my truck and on the road, I forget to call her back.

A news anchor blares out a headline, but I'm in a hurry, so I turn the volume down to a low murmur as I drive the cramped winding roads to the docks where the ferry should be waiting. If I'm lucky, they are running late and haven't gotten there yet. Taylor has to ride over with Emily and then take the last ferry out, so if they get there before I do, I'm sure to get an earful. If she misses her trip back, we'll be stuck on the island together, and neither of us wants to spend more time together than we need to.

The roads are more crowded than usual. It's like a mass exodus of cars and I have to fight in bumper to bumper traffic to get to the docks. You would think there was a celebrity coming to Rockaway Island, for Christ's sake. I didn't even know there were so many cars on the island.

It's the third helicopter that has my brain switching from panicked about being late, and pissing Taylor off, to alert and focused. When the traffic clears, I see three police cruisers parked haphazardly over the sidewalk and then dread balls up in my stomach like a hissing, venomous snake ready to attack me from the inside out.

In my career, intuition has always served me well. When you're in the middle of a gun fight, cornered, and don't know where to go, sometimes all you can do is trust your gut. So far, it hasn't led me wrong.

When ice forms in my chest and a cold sweat slicks my skin, even in the ninety-degree weather, I know something's wrong.

Then, I notice the helicopters. They weren't planes advertising free facials or declaring some idiots eternal love like I'd thought earlier. They were from the sheriff's department, and various television stations.

I slam my car into a parking stop, not giving a damn about the handicapped spot. *Fuck the fines.*

I spot Tyler's bald head above the crowd and elbow my way through the gawking spectators to where he stands with a dozen other uniformed cops. His expression when he finds me is grim. In all the years I've known him, I've never seen him look so devastated, including the night he had to deliver the news my parents were dead.

That's the second clue shit's about to go bad. Tyler can always be counted on to bring levity to any situation so when he's serious, everyone around him takes on the same energy. It's what makes him such a great cop, a great leader, and an even better friend.

By the time I reach his side, three more helicopters have flown overhead, and my anxiety has grown through the roof. All of the aerial activity is focused on one spot across the spit of ocean. The copters circle overhead like vultures and the distant whine of their beating blades reminds me a little too much of war in the Middle East.

As if it knows it, my body reacts without thought. My muscles go loose and wired, ready for action at a moment's notice. I pick up shreds of conversation from the crowd milling around the gathering of cops. All of my senses are on hyper-alert.

So when my phone goes off again, my heart threatens to jump out of my chest.

I turn to Tyler, who is still looking at me with a solemn expression on his worn features. For the first time since I've known him, he looks every day of his fifty years. "What's going on?"

He takes a moment to answer, then puts his hand on my

shoulder. Tyler's a great guy, a good friend, but he's not the type for physical affection between men.

"It's the ferry," he says. Then my phone rings again. "You should answer your phone."

My brows furrow as I try to puzzle out what one has to do with the other. I swipe a thumb over the unlock indicator and fifteen missed calls from Taylor appear on the screen. I open the voicemail and find a dozen or so messages blinking for my attention. They all last for a couple seconds at most.

Damn if my finger doesn't tremble when I swipe over the first message and hit play.

I raise the phone to my ears and all of the outside noise seems to fade away as the message plays.

Out of all the horrors I've witnessed and the atrocities I've committed, there has never been anything more terrifying in my life than the moment my daughter's voice screams, "Daddy!" in my ear.

CHLOE

The gunman directs the rest of us in line to get on the boat before we attract too much attention. He points the gun in each person's face and based on his own expression, he won't hesitate to use it at the first sign of reluctance.

The dock isn't empty, there are people milling about everywhere. People getting on and off their own boats in distant slips. Official looking attendants checking new patrons in and out.

Any of them could be a potential rescuer. But if I call out, what will happen?

I'll get shot, or they will, and then there will be more innocent people in danger. The little girl will still be way too damn close to a deadly weapon—or worse. I don't want to speculate about the possibilities, but it's hard not to.

Before I have another panic-stricken moment to think, the woman and her daughter reach the man with the gun. The girl is crying and when it's her turn to board the ferry, she freezes, her little pink tennis shoes clinging to the dock, and her small frame shaking. Her mother ferrets away the little phone behind her back as they get closer. Her daughter whimpers, shaking so hard I can hear her teeth clack together.

"Sweetie," her mother says with a tone of desperation. "C'mon, Emily." She tries to stay calm, tries to keep her emotions reigned in, but her voice breaks mid-sentence and her own tears slip down her cheeks.

"No, Mommy. I don't want to," she says. "I want Daddy." She clutches the little wolf like a lifeline and my heart twists inside my chest. "Daddy!" the little girl cries.

Her mother's face drains of all remaining color, but she manages to slip her phone into her pocket before bringing her trembling hands in front of her.

He says nothing, but his silence is enough. Like a dark, ominous storm cloud, he hovers over the trembling child and gestures with the gun for them to get a move on.

My hands are clammy and I can't get rid of the moisture collecting on my palms, even when I rub them against my dress. I don't want to draw attention to myself, I don't want the gun to jerk in my direction.

I learn a lot about myself in the following seconds, as I'm sure many do when confronted with life or death situations.

When the little girl doesn't take the step forward, her mother pleads with her in hushed tones, but to no avail. The gunman's face reddens, his eyes bouncing from face to face until he lands back on the girl. His attention is the last thing she needs if she's going to make it out of this alive.

He takes a step forward and jerks the mother away from her kid. She fights like a feral alley cat, clawing at his face and shrieking. She screams, drawing the attention of the people around us and faint sounds of alarm erupt at the sight of the gun. It's a surreal picture, seeing a gun in broad daylight with the sounds of happy families and boats, and the cheerful caw of sea birds in the background.

The man growls and then pushes the mother off the dock where she tumbles like a rag doll down into the choppy blue of the ocean, flipping once, moving all too fast and slow at the same time. Her scream cuts off with a loud *thunk* and a gurgle of water. A mushroom of red mixes with the froth left in her wake. She must have knocked against the dock or the boat. Either way, a couple seconds pass and she doesn't resurface. For one terrible second, I think she may be dead.

Forgetting the danger and the inevitable fatal repercussions, I scream to the nearest bystander who's close to where she fell. "Help her!" I point at the bubbles floating to the surface. "Help! Help her!"

Not one, but two men jump in after her. They either don't see or don't care about the man waving a gun. One of them gets an arm under her shoulders and swims her over to a ladder alongside the dock. I can't tell from the distance if she's breathing or not, but they've got her. They'll get her help. There's nothing else I can do for her. I push her limp body from my mind and zero in on the screaming little girl.

Her feet are glued to the planks as she cowers in front of the man, a tiny figure shadowed by his hulking form. Her little body shakes with the effort of her screams. Heads turn in our direction, and her scream resounds through the mouths of every person in the vicinity. Like osmosis, the alarm travels until everyone takes notice.

The people behind me take the chance at escape and flee while the gunman is focused on the little girl. I hear their footsteps slap against the sea-worn wooden planks. My feet itch to follow in their swift retreat, but I can't leave her alone.

I can't leave her alone.

Before I can second-guess my decision, I cross the space between us and move the girl's trembling body behind me.

"Leave her alone," I say. My heart is hammering its way through my chest and I can taste the salty essence of tears on my lips. I didn't even know I was crying.

He twitches a finger over the trigger and the sound of the safety flicking off echoes over the crash of the waves against the dock. I stumble backward, but he stops me with a growled, "Get on the boat."

I swallow around the knot in my throat. "L-let the little girl g-go," I say.

"Get on the boat," he repeats. "Both of you."

There are sirens behind us now and a very small part of me is clinging to the hope that, maybe, they can still save us, so I shake my head. "No. I'll go, but not until you let the little girl stay. Please, she's just a kid."

He fires a shot off to the side, and I shriek. The little girl behind me screams even louder, her cries almost unintelligible. My own sobs wrench their way through my chest.

Long seconds pass and I know he won't let her go. I make a split decision and walk forward with the little girl huddled close behind me. My skin flashes hot, then cold and I can't stop shaking, but I force myself to put one foot in front of the other, even though I'm shaking so hard it makes walking difficult.

When I get close enough he jerks me forward with a hand wrapped vice-like around my bicep. I trip over my own feet and collide with his chest. That's when I realize he doesn't look terrifying at all. Instead, he reminds me of my grandpa before he got sick with cancer and wasted away in a hospital bed. He's not old, just older.

His salt and pepper mustache and beard are neatly trimmed and his matching hair closely shorn. He doesn't look like a person I'd expect to wave around a gun and threaten little children, and it almost makes his actions all the worse. He should be at home with his wife watching football and complaining about the weather.

All of it flashes through my head as his arms wrap around me. In an instant, I realize this may be my one chance to get the little girl to safety, so I wrap my hands around him like I'm trying to catch my balance.

While he's distracted, I twist my head around and shout at the stunned little girl, "Run! Go!"

She stands there stupefied and wide-eyed for a few seconds, and then she's off, streaking back down the length of the dock and into the waiting arms of strangers who form a human shield around her little body. My last image of her is the little stuffed wolf still clutched in her hand.

I'm so relieved to find her safe, I collapse into his arms. His angry shout pulls me from the bout of momentary relief and then fear shrouds me in a cold blanket once more.

He thrusts me toward the ferry and I fall hard on my knees. I cry out and he shoves me forward with a booted foot and then jumps the rest of the way. The crowd of people already trapped on the ferry watch as he rolls me to my back with his foot.

"You shouldn't have done that," he says.

I shouldn't have. I'm sure it's the #1 rule in every manual about hostage situations: don't engage the hostile party. Keep quiet and stay out of his way and whatever you do, don't make yourself a target.

So much for smart thinking, Chloe.

But I can't find it in me to regret my spur of the moment decision. If I die today, at least I know I did it protecting an innocent little girl.

He tears his cold, blue eyes off my prone form and shouts up to the top deck, "Get this heap moving now or I'll use these people down here for target practice!"

When no one moves, he rips the zipper from his nondescript black jacket and reveals a vest strapped with several weapons.

Someone is moving behind me, but I can't tear my eyes away from the guns.

This can't be happening.

The ferry inches away from the dock and the man directs everyone to move inside the main floor where the walls are lined with benches. Someone helps me to my feet and I limp my way to a spot as far away from his imposing figure as I can.

Water yawns in the space between the ferry and the dock and there's nothing but open sea and the sliver of Rockaway Island in the distance.

I put my head between my knees and pray for the first time in my life.

Because now it's me who needs saving.

CHAPTER THREE

GABRIEL

ONE MINUTE I have the phone in my hand and the next I'm diving at Tyler's cruiser, trying to wrestle the keys out of his hand. Tunnel vision blocks out everything but the result: get to my daughter.

I don't have time for obstacles. Tyler and I have been friends for a long time, I smash my fist into his face when he tackles me to the ground. I feel no pain, but I hear the *crack* of bone against bone. His mouth is moving, but I can't hear over the ringing in my ears.

We tumble over the scorching blacktop until Tyler manages to pin me down. The asphalt burns the exposed skin on my back and arms, but I ignore it and focus on getting his bulk off of me.

"Calm down, goddammit!" he shouts in my face. "Christ, Gabe, *listen to me!*"

"I swear to fucking God, Ty, if you don't get off me right now I'll do something we'll both regret."

His meaty arms wrap around my neck and he holds me down in an effective—and irritating—chokehold. "I said, listen."

"Fuck!" My voice is hoarse from the pressure of his forearm against my throat. "All right, say what you're going to say so I can go, but hurry the fuck up about it."

Tyler studies me. "If I let you up are you going to sucker punch me again?"

"I'm not gonna make any promises," I say.

He spits out a mouthful of blood on the concrete next to me. "Fair enough."

He gets to his feet and helps me up. A crowd of officers press in around us, but Tyler waves them away. He pulls me to the open door of his cruiser and shoves me into the driver's seat. "There's a gunman with an estimated ten to fifteen hostages on the ferry, but your daughter is safe."

A wave of welcome relief crashes over me. The allaying of guilt and fear is so monumental, betraying tears sting my eyes. Tyler presses a hand to my shoulder until I suck it up. When I speak, my voice is still hoarse, though not from Tyler's very effective methods of restraint. "Where is she?"

"She's at the hospital with Taylor."

Guilt assaults me again because I didn't even think about her. What kind of fucking man am I? "Is—" my throat closes around the words. "Is Taylor okay?"

Tyler nods. "She's fine. Little bump on the head, possible

concussion, but otherwise, she and Emily are very lucky. Get in the car. They'll fly us over so you can see her."

I slide across the bench seat to the passenger side and Tyler follows me. The air inside the car is too cool and I shiver even though it's gotta be a hundred degrees outside. "Explain."

Tyler shifts with ease and backs out of the parking lot, tires squealing. "There isn't much information as the story is still developing. All we know is an armed man boarded the ferry about a half hour ago. There was a struggle and Taylor was thrown off the dock. She hit her head on the way down."

"Jesus Christ," I bite out.

"Two witnesses say another woman shielded Emily from the perp. They say she saved her from becoming a hostage."

We make it across the island in record time. Rockaway isn't big to begin with, but Tyler breaks every speed limit on the way to the small helipad we have for emergencies. He doesn't bother parking in the designated spots and we dash out of the car to the waiting pilot.

"You Gabriel Rossi?" he asks. I nod and he gestures to the back, "Get in."

Tyler follows close behind me, but as soon as we get in, I focus on the space in front of us and he fades to my periphery, im-fucking-patient to get to my daughter.

The beat of the helicopter blades drowns out anything else and then we're lifting up off the ground and moving forward. My stomach drops and once again I'm transported back to the desert where I spent the majority of my time traveling back and forth in the choppy carriage of a helicopter. I have to focus on the cool blue of the water below and the salt in the wind coming in through the open sides to keep from having a bitch of a flashback.

Emily needs me now. She's what matters.

The ride across the channel between the coast of Florida and the island is mercifully short. Soon, we touch down atop the hospital and I jump out running. A pair of officers greet me at the rooftop entrance and lead me down a flight of dark stairs to a bustling hospital floor. I don't even have to ask where to go before they lead me to a bank of elevators.

A police officer puts a reassuring hand on my shoulder before the elevator doors swing open to chaos. I nod to him in thanks before I'm enveloped by a sea of nurses. A young, male doctor leads the pack and rushes to my side.

"Mr. Rossi, this way." He elbows his way through the crowd and leads me down a hall of doors. "Mrs. Rossi is awake, but weak. Her condition is stable."

Thank God. "And my daughter?"

"She's here. Your wife's mother is watching her."

I don't bother correcting him and by the time I think to, we're arriving at a closed door. The doctor pushes it open and reveals a frail-looking Taylor hooked up to monitors and Emily asleep beside her in the hospital bed.

Tears fill Taylor's red-rimmed eyes and trail down her cheeks. "Gabe." When her voice breaks she reaches for tissues and covers her face, her shoulders trembling.

I leave the doctor in the doorway and fall to my knees by

her bedside. Even with as much animosity as there's been between us during our divorce, I'm reminded I've been inside this woman. She's been *by* my side, a friend, for years. We may have our moments of anger, but we married each other for a reason. I loved her then, and still care for her now. The part of me who stood by her side for four years burns to annihilate the man who hurt her.

"I'm here." I don't know what to do with my hands. The side of her face is black and blue where it must have connected with the dock. There's a bandage taped from her temple to her chin. "I'm here. I'm sorry."

Her hand comes to my cheek, and I lean into it. Wires trail down from a clip on her finger to a beeping machine. "Shh. Don't be sorry."

"I should have been there." I kiss her palm and then take it between my hands. "I'm sorry I was late. You were right. You're always right. I shouldn't put other people in front of my family. I should have been there," I repeat, this time with a trace of anger.

She shakes her head, winces, then licks her chapped lips. "Don't say that." I press my head over our clasped hands and will the waves of emotions back. "Don't ever say that. I didn't realize before what it meant to you to rescue everyone." At her words, my eyes lift to hers. "I didn't realize how important people like you are. That if you weren't rescuing people, no one would. I wish I'd never given you such a hard time."

"You don't have to apologize," I tell her. "You should rest."

"Let me get this out before they come back with more

drugs and I'm too tired to finish it." She wipes away a tear with her free hand. "The woman who saved Emily, there won't be any way for me to repay her. And I realized when I woke up she reminds me of you. If you were there, you would have done the same thing. You would have put yourself in front of a man with a gun without a second thought." Taylor cups my cheek and lifts my eyes to hers. "Our daughter is lucky to have a man like you for a father. And I'm lucky to have you for a friend."

My shoulders heave and I have to suck in hot, humid gulps of air as emotions assail me. Taylor's hands sift through my hair until I can control myself.

By the time I stand, straight-faced, Emily is stirring awake. I lean a hip on the side of the bed and hold Taylor's hand in mine. When her eyes open, Emily finds me and smiles.

"Daddy, you're here!" She climbs across her mother's legs and launches herself into my arms. "I'm so glad to see you."

"I'm so glad to see you, too." If I were standing my knees would have buckled. I close my eyes and press my face into her hair until the emotion causing my arms to tremble diminishes. When I let her go, I say, "What do you say we break out of here and get your mom a milkshake?" To Taylor, I say, "Is chocolate still your favorite?"

They both look at me with identical frowns.

A crease forms between my eyebrows. "What? Don't tell me you like vanilla now."

"You can't mean to say you're planning to stay here?" Taylor purses her lips in a familiar expression.

"Yeah, Daddy, you have to go save her."

"Uh, save who?" I narrow my eyes at the pair of them.

Emily scoffs and waves an arm. "That lady."

I look at Taylor for backup, but she's giving me a look identical to Emily's, a mix of frustration and confusion.

"What?" I rub the back of my neck and wonder where the hell all the nurses are.

"The woman who helped Emily, Gabe," Taylor explains finally. "You can't just leave her after what she did."

"Yea, Daddy. You told me you saved people from bad things."

"There are other policemen and a lot of other trained professionals who will help the people on the ferry," I explain with measured patience.

"But Mommy said you're the best." Emily's blue eyes shine up at me, and they are filled with a pride and admiration I'm not sure I live up to.

Taylor smiles at me when I glance at her. Then I look at my daughter and say "I don't think it's a good idea for me to leave you now."

"Daddy," Emily says, then presses her lips into a firm line like I'm the child and she's the adult. "I'm fine. But the lady isn't."

"My mom's with us," Taylor says and at the mention of her name, her mother comes to stand by her side. We'd gotten along, barely, when Taylor and I were married, but for the first time, she looks at me without disgust. "You should be there," Taylor is saying. "You know you want to be."

Emily grins and squeezes my hand. "Go, Daddy."

I cup her cheek and kiss her forehead. "You're sure about this?" My eyes meet Taylor's over our daughter's head.

"More than anything. She risked her life for Emily. The least you can do is try to save hers."

CHLOE

There are thirteen other people on this boat, heading God-knows-where, including the captain still driving the ferry and the attendants who are huddled in their blue button-up uniforms. The man with the guns strapped to his chest and back like a vest full of bombs—and just as lethal—has said nothing to anyone other than giving the captain vague directions.

From what I can see, we're going at a low speed, based on the distance between us and the shore. I can still see miniature people at the dock where I'd saved the little girl, except now there are scores of policemen, paramedics, and journalists. Their lights flicker like a funhouse ride and I can hear the occasional whir of a helicopter overhead.

So far, no one has tried to contact us via the onboard radio, and the man hasn't attempted to open a line of communication.

But what's worse than his threatening presence is the tension between the hostages.

Beside me, a woman huddles with her two children, her husband hovers nearby, his face angry with a combination of indignation and fear. Every few minutes he mutters something under his breath about *doing something about this shit* and I want to slap my hand over his mouth—not that I have much room to talk.

Just a short while ago, I myself *did something about it* and wound up as a hostage on a boat in the middle of the Atlantic with a gun pointed at my face. So I'm content to sit in my little corner with my head down and my lips zipped unless I have to do otherwise. The others around me, however, don't feel the same.

"You might want to sit down," I whisper through the corner of my mouth. *So much for keeping your lips zipped.*

The mother's eyes dart in my direction, harden. "If it weren't for you, we wouldn't be in this position," she hisses.

I jerk back and suck in an involuntary gasp. "Lady, he was gonna take you with or without my help."

She doesn't say anything. Just glowers in return.

The ferry is a monstrous two-story structure with an underfloor compartment where the engines are housed. On the main level are the benches for passengers and two rows along the outside full of cars, their drivers peer through with wide-eyes. They don't get out and they don't unlock their doors. I wouldn't either. A pane of glass and a door panel might not be much, but it at least provides them a shred of protection from the destructive path of a bullet.

The top level features an observation deck and the small squat room where the captain maneuvers the boat. Because there's nowhere else for us to go, the man with the gun paces up there with his eyes on the horizon.

I don't know what he's waiting for and I'm not sure if I want to find out.

The sun is sinking in the distance, and more than anything, I don't want to be stranded on this boat with a madman as we drift on the ocean through the dark nothingness.

As soon as the coast of Jacksonville is but a sliver in the distance and the refuge of the island still far away, the gunman appears at the top of the stairs. His dark, beady eyes sift through the hostages until they land on me and recognition flairs. Ice solidifies in my stomach.

"You there," he says and points the handgun at me. "C'mere."

I could look around to see if he is talking to someone else, but I don't have the bravado in me anymore to play stupid. Once the little girl was safe and the promise of refuge and rescue diminished, all the nerve propelling me to leap at an armed man leached away.

Now I'm just cold all over. Even though it's a humid Florida evening, the slight chill coming off the water wracks me from the inside out. The shivers get worse as I get to my feet and cross the lower level to the gray stairs leading to the top. The man waits for me with the gun pointed right at my head the whole time.

He twitches the gun to the side where the captain is

steering the ferry with hands white-knuckled on the wheel. "Take the wheel," he says.

The captain glances over and opens his mouth to object, then closes it when he realizes this is not the time. Without a word, I do as he says.

The wheel is still warm from the captain's hands. My own grip the heated plastic and I struggle to keep hold with limp fingers. I don't want to touch the things he's touched. Bile rises in my throat and my toes curl in my shoes to drive the thoughts from my brain. I've never driven a boat before, especially not one even half this size, but when there's a gun in your face, you'll do pretty much whatever the person holding it asks you to.

There's a strangled cry behind me and when I glance back, the gunman has the captain on his knees.

"Hey," I shout, when he twists the captain's arms behind his back.

The gunman looks up at me, his eyes narrow slits. "You're gonna wanna keep those hands on the wheel, little lady. Wouldn't want you to run aground and have all these lives on your conscience."

Reminding myself it's best to keep my mouth shut, I press my lips together and focus on the empty sea in front of me. The pained gasps and grunts from behind me are so hard to listen to, I try to block them out. I can't cover my ears because I need my hands to drive and I'm too afraid to hum, so I try to picture something, anything, to take me out of this moment.

As much as I try to draw the image of my family to mind, it doesn't work.

I have to knot my fingers around the wheel to keep from interfering. To think I was the type of person who couldn't confront an ex-boyfriend just a few short hours ago and now I'm jumping at each opportunity to throw myself in front of danger.

The next time I look back, I find the gunman has restrained the captain with his arms behind his back and then affixed a necklace of sorts around his neck. Then I realize, it's not a necklace at all.

It's a collar filled with explosives.

The captain is physically fit for an older guy of around sixty. His full head of white hair reminds me of Santa Claus along with his red cheeks.

He shouldn't be here. None of us should be here.

"Hand me the radio, darlin'," the gunman gestures to the handheld microphone dangling from a hook up and to my right. When he's not shouting orders, he sounds like such a normal guy. Not someone I should be terrified of and yet I'm terrified all the same.

I give over the radio, and he flicks the channel to the announcement system so his next words are broadcast to everyone onboard.

"Everyone needs to line up by the benches on the lower deck on their knees with their hands behind their backs. If you're in a vehicle, please exit the vehicle at this time. I repeat, line up on the lower deck on your knees with your hands behind your back."

Almost immediately, I hear the people below rushing about to do as he instructs.

Then, I sense his presence draw near. His fingers lift the long length of my hair and drape it over my shoulder. Detached from the situation, I observe the distinct scent of mint chewing gum as he wraps a length of cord around my neck.

When he's done, he closes a lock around the ends at the back, and I know this day just went from bad—to worse.

CHAPTER FOUR

GABRIEL

"THE HELL YOU ARE," is the first thing Tyler says when I explain the situation in the hospital hallway.

Emily and Taylor both fell asleep a short while after making their demands, and I left them in the quiet but capable control of my ex-mother-in-law. For some reason, she seems to like me more now than she ever did when I was married to her daughter. But God help me if I try to understand why.

Nurses part around Tyler and me as we argue in the middle of the hallway. I try to move over so they can pass, but Tyler grips my arm to keep me from getting away.

His genial expression is replaced with a glower. "Don't give me that look," I say.

Tyler shakes his head. "I'll give you whatever look I damn well please when you're talking stupid, boy."

"This woman saved my family, Ty. My family. The least I can do is go down there and rip down some of the red tape."

He lets out an exasperated sigh. "Speaking as your friend and not in an official capacity at all, there is no way in hell the suits will let you tag along with their operation this time. This isn't a search and rescue. This is an active hostage situation. The big guys in Jacksonville have it handled."

"Then we'll just push a few buttons, feel the situation out. I'm sure they've got it handled. I owe it to my daughter."

"And when that doesn't work?"

"It will."

"If it doesn't," he says, "then I want your promise you won't do anything stupid. You may be a grunt but this isn't Afghanistan. You don't get to wage war here."

"Consider it a peaceful operation," I say.

"You're incapable of peaceful operations," he mutters under his breath.

As we head downstairs to a waiting Jacksonville police car, I clap a hand on his shoulder and say, "That's the nicest thing you've ever said."

The sidewalk outside the hospital is packed with reporters looking for a juicy story, but Ty and I keep our heads down until we're inside the cruiser. Lights flash outside the windows and cameras click against the glass as the masses press in for their scoop until we leave them looking defeated behind us.

It's a short ride to the marina where a small command center is stationed. Uniformed police guard the perimeter and cops in pressed suits hunch over schematics under bright lights.

Tyler flashes his identification and gets us under the tape. A badge sits in the corner with a radio attempting to rouse the hostage taker on the ferry with no success.

Tyler introduces himself to the man in charge, who says his name is Chief Stevens. "If you need anything at all on our end please don't hesitate."

"Thank you," Stevens responds. "We'll do that."

"This is Gabriel Rossi, former Marine Recon. He volunteers with Coast Guard Search and Rescue. His daughter was the one the woman saved."

Stevens nods and shakes my hand.

"I'd like to help out in any way I can, sir," I say.

"I appreciate it, son. But we've got it handled."

Tyler gives me an *I told you so* look, but I nod at them both so I don't betray my real intentions. Stevens doesn't look like he'd be slow on the uptake and I'd hate to have to kick his ass. "Ty, if you don't mind, I'll have them take me back to the hospital."

"We could use you here to coordinate," Stevens says to Tyler.

Ty gives me a pained look.

"Don't worry," I tell him. "Going straight there."

"Selena will have your hide if you do something stupid."

I nod but I say nothing else. I don't have any time to waste. The trip back to the hospital passes in a blur. I don't give the helicopter pilot any room to argue and instruct he takes me back to the island.

Night is falling below us, and the ferry is illuminated by its onboard lights, a beacon in the otherwise obsidian sea. On both coasts, emergency response vehicles and their operators perch like stalwart guardians, their lights rain down on the water like carnival lights and sprays of fireworks.

The helicopter touches down on the helipad where Tyler's car still waits where he left it. The whole island is quiet, like everyone is holding a collective breath until the tragedy has passed.

I use the keys I'd snagged from Tyler with a silent apology as I crank and steer the cruiser back to my house.

Based on snatches of conversation from their headquarters, a rescue effort will begin within an hour unless contact is made with the captor, which won't bode well for the hostages. If interrupted it's much more likely the night will end in bloodshed.

I park the cruiser behind a copse of squat palm trees and unlock my house. Rudy greets me with a loud yap. I let him out of his cage and he sprints out to piss, then follows me into my workshop where I store my gear.

There's no telling what kind of situation I'll be getting myself into, so I spare nothing. I change into a serviceable wetsuit and water shoes, then shoulder my gear.

The dock is quiet as I slip into the shadows of night, except for the distant buzz of activity. Water laps against the side of my boat and I drop my bag in the passenger seat. The engine turns over with a gentle purr.

An immediate calm settles over me as I navigate through the dark water. I keep my lights on low not wanting to attract attention.

There's a chill coming off the water since the sun has gone down. I have my suit to protect me but a civilian wouldn't. The cold may not be enough to kill them outright but it wouldn't help their chances of survival if they get tossed over.

When I get close enough to see the outline of the ferry in the darkness, I cut my lights and allow my eyes to adjust to the lack of light.

Silence.

It's not a good sign. Neither is the fact that the captor hasn't contacted negotiators.

While my boat idles in view of the ferry, I pull out my binoculars to study the activity on the boat. There isn't much to see at first, but I'm patient.

I notice movement on the lower deck. I refocus and find a mass of people huddled together on the bottom floor. They're all on their knees with their hands behind their backs.

From the significant distance, I can't make out a threat with any certainty, so I inch the boat as close as I can without arousing suspicion. Once I'm close enough to make out more detail I find the majority of hostages gathered on the floor.

I don't assume there aren't more because assumptions in any dangerous situation never end well.

When I find no one threatening on the first level, I raise my gaze to the second.

And that's when I find her.

My daughter described her as a princess and even across the space between us, I couldn't agree more. She's the type of woman who should be in a man's bed being pampered, not crying anguished tears with a madman hovering behind her.

What the hell is she doing there?

I put down my binoculars and maneuver my boat around the back of the ferry. Based on diagrams I've got, there is a hatch to access the back of the engine room on the lowest level. My best chance at accessing the ferry undetected will be there, provided the asshole has no extra surveillance set up.

Either way, I'll to be ready for anything he has planned.

I'm coming for you, asshole.

CHLOE

The collar itself isn't uncomfortable like I thought it would be. It resembles dozens of other necklaces I've chosen myself, though much heavier. I wonder how he constructed an explosive on such a small scale. Then I think about whether or not it will effectively mutilate its intended victims.

Then I stop thinking about it altogether.

I gaze out the front window and try to ignore the man with the weapons chaining people to their death. I've never had the luxury of taking cruises—I've never given myself the time off from work, let alone had enough money left over from bills to save for one of the main cruise liners operating out of Jacksonville.

But if I could have, I imagine it would be something like this. The gentle lapping of the water against the side. The constant magical sound of waves in the distance and night air laden with salt and sea.

If I don't think too hard about the circumstances, the night could almost be beautiful.

Almost.

He hasn't told me where to go, so I keep the ferry moving in the same direction the captain was going before I took over. On this course, we'll surpass Rockaway Island and head right out into the Atlantic, going southwest toward Miami. At least, that's what the navigation panel in front of me says.

Every few minutes, I can't resist glancing back as he works down the morbid line of people. His face is calm, impassive, almost methodical as he works with each person. He's not aggressive. In fact, he doesn't say a word as he strings each of them up with their own collar of explosives.

A flash, at least, I think it's a flash, draws my attention to the left side of the ferry. I squint my eyes in the general direction.

Is it another boat?

God, that would be too easy, wouldn't it? The cops will come in, subdue the bad guy and then we can all go home. Hope rises on delicate wings in my chest.

A rescue party would be too much to hope for. I have to

tell myself to keep from experiencing the crushing disappointment that's sure to come if it's not.

I search the water, eyes straining to make out the flash again from churning white caps in the distance. There's nothing of course, just water, useless water.

"You surprise me again," comes a voice from behind me.

Cursing underneath my breath, I glance over my shoulder and find him standing just behind me. I chastise myself for becoming so distracted I didn't notice the man creeping up behind me.

For an older guy he moves like a panther.

Silent...and lethal.

"I'm not sure I want to know what surprises you."

Then he surprises *me* by chuckling. He taps the dash. "Just keep it straight, just like this, and we won't have any problems."

I nod because I don't trust myself to speak.

"Good girl." He grabs the radio with one meaty hand, probably for another morbid-ass announcement.

I clench my hands on the wheel to keep from doing anything crazy, like jumping on his back and beating my fists against his head.

While he's distracted by twisting the knobs on the radio, I peek at the captain, who's slumped over on the floor between a crate and the wall of controls. He doesn't look too injured, but he's old, even older than our abductor. His bald head is glossy with sweat. It drips over his closed eyes and down his ashen cheeks, despite the chilling breeze coming off the water.

The radio squeals, then clears. The chatter below us ceases. "Good evening, passengers. This is your captain speaking." He smiles a little and then continues, "As long as you follow my instructions carefully, no one will get hurt today. Stay calm, don't cause a fuss and we'll all go home safely." He looks at me during the next part, and his black eyes are as frigid as the night air. "But if you attempt to get off this boat. If you attempt to harm me, the collars you're wearing will decapitate you so fast, your body won't even know what happened."

I resist the desire to pull at the constrictive rubber around my neck. My mind is screaming at me to get it off, get it off, *get it off* in an endless refrain. Sweat pops out on my skin with the effort it takes to keep my hands on the wheel. Each time I swallow my throat bobs against the restriction. Even though I know I can breathe, it's getting harder and harder to choke down the briny air.

Before the man can continue his instructions, commotion on the lower floor pulls our attention down. The man takes a few steps, stretching the cord along behind him. I risk keeping one hand on the wheel to peer around the corner so I can see down the stairs.

I see blood first and my initial thought is the man shot someone, but then the two men fighting come into view, one of them with a bloody nose.

It's the father. The one who is so pissed off.

He must be pushed to his limit because he clocks the guy trying to restrain him.

The man beside me shakes his head and sets down the

radio. I have a fleeting thought to use it to contact someone on shore, but I gulp and remember defying the gunman would be a terrible idea.

There's another shout and the father shoves the guy trying to pin him down. The guy trips over his own feet and momentum carries him right over a line of wire guarding the edges of the ferry's side.

His hoarse cry follows him over the edge.

Everyone on board holds a collective breath. After a few seconds, when nothing happens, the buzz of low conversation reaches my ears. I hear snippets like *where is he? Did the bomb not go off? What's going on?*

From my vantage point, I can only see a slice of water just over the top of the ceiling of the bottom floor. Since it's dark, the ocean there is just a swirling mass of blackness. With one hand on the wheel, I stretch to my tippy toes to catch a glimpse of the man who's fallen overboard.

Maybe his collar was defective. Maybe this crazy man has no idea what he's doing.

Maybe we'll make it out of this alive.

For someone who just threatened a boatful of people with decapitation if they tried to escape, the man beside me seems calm. Too calm.

A thread of discord sews the lining of my stomach.

This is gonna be bad.

The father down below, realizing what he's done, gets to his feet and lurches toward the back to go after the man in the water. He must spot him because he reaches out an arm, but he has to know there's no way he can get him back.

After a few seconds of futile rescue attempts, he spots one of those red and white floats they throw over the side for just this purpose. Snagging it, he tosses it over the edge. The bobbing float edges into my view and then a dark shape hovers over it.

Relief has me swaying and I have to hold onto the wheel to keep from sinking into a pile on the floor.

It's chaos on the bottom deck. A woman who must be his girlfriend is screaming. The father's kids are wailing; one is sobbing so hard he can't breathe. Their mother tries to calm them down, but she's crying too hard to get the words out.

But it's nothing, *nothing*, compared to the eruption of mayhem from below when the man holding the float explodes.

CHAPTER FIVE

GABRIEL

She looks right at me.

With my boat lights extinguished and my wetsuit and gear dark blue or black, she can't *see* me. If she could, then he could, and then all hell will break loose.

But I see her.

I should look for entry points and weaknesses in his defense, but I can't tear my eyes away from the silvery trail of tears down her cheeks. Her black hair is windswept and pulled back from her face into a hasty bun. Pieces of it are falling down around her bare shoulders. She seems far too delicate to have a man with a gun standing behind her.

A pool of shadows obscure his face and getting in any closer to make out any detail will blow my cover. So I sit, and I wait for my opening. The last thing the people on the ferry need is for me to go charging in without gathering information first. Though with her innocent face and gut wrenching tears as a beacon in the darkness, I'm sure as hell tempted to charge in guns blazing.

I put in my ear piece and tune the channel so I can listen in to the emergency response teams relaying information to each other. I gather from their relentless squawking there's been no contact from the ferry.

Which isn't a good sign. If he isn't making any demands, then he could just be in it for the grand finale.

And if that's the case then I'll get to him before he sets it in motion.

Getting on the boat undetected will require a little bit of finesse, but I'm well used to operating in the water. I've been on or around the water in some aspect my whole life.

The adrenaline surging through my system when I saw the police waiting at the ferry entrance faded by the time I was leaving the hospital after I spoke with Emily and Taylor. A steady calm replaced it once I gathered my familiar gear, checking and double checking my supplies.

Now, I'm settled into the familiar place that allows me to prioritize tasks and mete out justice on my own terms. It doesn't even occur to me to consider I don't have orders for this particular mission, and I'm pretty sure the proper authorities will be incensed when they find me onboard the ferry after they specifically told me to leave it alone.

I pop in a piece of spearmint gum as I bob on the water about a hundred yards to the northeast of their position. The tail end of conversations and screaming and crying reach me.

The offender is on the top deck speaking to the pretty woman with the black hair.

Their body language tells me she's afraid of him, but not so much that she lets him intimidate her into cowering away. She's a fighter, this one. The thought makes me grin a little around my piece of gum. Emily would like her, if they met under different circumstances. Taylor, too, probably. Lord knows the two of them give me enough trouble.

I'll owe her a beer, hell, maybe even my grandma's secret recipe for lasagna, when all this is over. Emily had made me promise to bring her rescuer over to see her.

Now how will I go about doing that?

My best bet will be the waist high rail located at the back of the boat. At the opportune moment, I can snake along the back and hide in between the cars for cover until I figure out my next move.

I can't weigh anchor this close to the ferry. Otherwise, he may see and suspect something. I don't need him knocking off hostages because of a stupid mistake, so I guide my boat a way out, until I'm sure it's cloaked in shadows. Unfortunately, this means the swim from my location to the boat will be one hell of a workout, even with my handheld propulsion device.

After I make sure the boat is secure, I strap on my diving gear and tuck my bag strap around my shoulders. The fall back into the water is a welcome one.

Yeah, I could panic. Everyone does at some point when under extreme pressure. Instead of devolving into a quivering, pathetic piece of shit, I channel my energy into focus. Like I've trained to do.

The propulsion machine pulls me through the water like a slick little dolphin until I can see the froth mixed up from the ferry's wake. Spying it, I dump the propulsion machine and work through the water with powerful strokes.

By the time I get to the boat's edge, my muscles are well oiled and I'm ready for the fight I know will come. I spit out the mouthpiece and peer up at the side, looking for the best place to climb up.

There's next to nothing on the side for me to grab onto. I'm as fit as the next gym rat former Marine, but there's no way for me to climb up a wall with no foot or handholds.

Shit.

I swipe a hand across my face to clear the rivulets of salt-water. There's an obtrusion on the side so I grab hold, if only to keep from getting left behind, while I sort out how to shinny up the side.

Then I hear the man take over the mic and my insides turn to ice. Blood rushing in my ears blocks out the beginning of his speech, but I catch the, "...if you attempt to get off this boat. If you attempt to harm me, the collars you're wearing will decapitate you so fast, your body won't even know what happened."

My fingers go limp and I slide back into the water. It rushes up my nose and stings my throat. I claw my way back to the handhold but his words still haunt me.

What would I have done if the woman hadn't saved Emily?

It doesn't take me long to figure he's got them all strapped with an explosive. My vision whites out when I think about Emily in just this situation so I push thoughts of her from my mind.

When'd you turn into such a fuckin' pussy, Rossi? I hear Tyler say in my ear.

It's enough to make me focus. Em isn't here. She's miles away surrounded by armed guards and I know her mother would fight to death to keep her safe. *Hell, she almost had.*

Over the sound of the water rushing around me and the hum and vibration from the engine, I hear the distinct sound of fist meeting face and a male cry of surprise. Are they trying to take on an armed man by themselves? It would take balls, even for a trained individual like me.

From the shouts going on above me, I'm able to deduce it's two of the passengers, one who *wants* to take on their captor and another who's trying to save the dude's life.

In stressful situations it's difficult to keep you're cool. I'm not surprised there's tension running through them. I just hope one of them doesn't do something stupid and get a lot of people killed before I can stop them.

But it happens too fast.

One of the men goes flying over the edge of the boat and I recall the kidnapper's last words. If he wasn't bluffing, the explosives strapped to the guy's neck will go off. It's just a matter of time.

Once he hits the water, I've already decided I don't have the time nor the opportunity to save him. And it's one of the hardest things I've ever had to do—to clutch the side of the boat and stay out of his sight.

"Help!" he shouts, his voice garbled by the water.

"Someone throw him a float!" another person yells.

There's the sound of wet footsteps, then a slap of an object hitting the water. Around the corner, I can hear the man thrashing in the water as he attempts to swim to the safety device.

He may make it before the device around his neck detonates—and it's the only chance he'll get.

When there's a moment of pause and it doesn't go off, I let out the breath I've been holding. Which is when it all goes to shit.

The explosion is enough to wrench me away from my hold on the ferry and toss me a couple feet. It rips the pack clean off my shoulders and my fingers grasp at empty water when I attempt to get it back.

Fuck.

I fight my way back to my hand hold again and shake my head to clear it of the ringing report from the explosion. I don't want to think about what's floating with me in the surrounding ocean. I'll think about it, dream about it, live with it, later. That and the fact he was right there. I could have saved him, but chose not to.

His death is on me.

I give myself a moment to refocus on my goal: getting on

the ship. Then I open my eyes. Above the ringing, I can hear the horrified screams of the other hostages.

If I was waiting on a distraction, this is it.

Then, I see the rope attached to a float that's no longer dangling from the end.

Looks like I've found my way on the boat after all.

CHLOE

There are no more tears. Just a numbing emptiness.

It doesn't dull my other senses—I can still hear the screams from below, can still feel the breeze on my face, and the shudder of the ferry beneath my hands, and smell the tang of metal and grease over the ocean.

But I can't handle all the rest so I tuck it in a box and stow it deep, deep inside my mind until the time comes when I can take it out and freak out properly.

Like never.

There was a part of me that hoped this guy was an irate employee using scare tactics in revenge of some corporate slight, but not anymore. The level of cold rage evident in the harsh downturn of his mouth speaks to a vendetta more personal than job termination.

Which doesn't bode well for me—or the other passengers.

Back toward shore, I can see the faint flashing lights from the emergency response, but the more we travel in the other direction, the farther away they—and safety—feel.

The man talks to the other passengers over the PA system

again, but a low beeping sound distracts me from whatever threats or demands he's making of them. I have to search the desk with all the displays for a while before I find the source of the sound. There are screens and monitors for everything, most of which I can't even understand.

The monitor beeping seems to show our current depth. It reminds me of one my grandpa used to have on his boat when we went fishing. It would show if there were any fish or obstructions beneath us. There must be something beneath us, near our tail end.

I only wish I were fishing instead of taken hostage.

There's a rope dangling off the end that must have been the remnants of the rescue attempt, which reminds me of the man. I shake my head of those thoughts.

But the odd thing is the rope is still swaying like there's something attached to it. Which has to be the wind.

"I'm sorry about that," I hear the man saying over the intercom. "Now I don't want any of you to get hurt, and you won't as long as you follow my directions."

I hope he knows none of us are fooled by his attempts to be friendly with us. We all know his promises are a crock. We're a means to an end to him. Something to bargain for his demands.

As he continues, reminding them about the rules: stay on the boat, don't fight him, I study the little bit of rope still rocking from side to side. There's something odd about it I can't put my finger on.

Then I realize: it's not swaying with the boat. It's going in the opposite direction.

There's something on the other end.

My thoughts are assailed with gruesome images of body parts hanging from the other side and I have to close my eyes and think about all my happy memories to blot them out.

Sienna, my family, my apartment. God, my life seems so boring in comparison, but now I fear I may never get back to it, I want nothing more than to live sixty years of boring.

Once I have control of my thoughts, I open my eyes and find a pair staring right back at me. I have to blink multiple times to make sure it's not a terrible waking nightmare. Then I realize I'm not imagining things. There's a man hanging from the rope.

People mention emotion or relief bringing them to their knees, but I've never understood the expression until the moment our eyes lock.

I can't discern much about him through the shadows and dark clothing, but he's here. He's going to help us. That's all I can think about.

He's here to help us.

A sound escapes my throat, and our captor stops in the middle of his speech to look sideways at me with raised brows. I cover the sound with a garbled cry and turn away from him, hoping he mistakes my gasp of surprise for choked tears.

Smooth, Chloe. Get the guy killed before he's even on the ferry.

I study the darkness in front of me as I pretend to get a

leash on my emotions. The man goes back to his speech and a few seconds later, I risk a glance to the back of the boat.

He's not there and for a second I wonder if I conjured him from a petrified place in my head. Then I see a wet trail leading from the back to my right side. He climbed up while the man was distracted looking at me.

I don't want to draw more attention to him, so I stare without seeing at the space in front of me. My spine is ramrod straight, my vision is blurry and my eyes sting from the strain.

The man's finished his tirade and his steps come close, though I don't want to turn to look at him for fear my expression will betray my thoughts. I've never been very good at lying. He hands me the radio and I cringe inwardly when our hands graze.

"Use this," he says. "Radio the Coast Guard, whoever, I don't care. Tell them you want to speak to whoever is in charge of emergency operations. Then tell them the only person I will speak with is Gabriel Rossi."

Then he leaves with nothing else by way of an explanation. I guess the gun prevents him from having to explain himself.

I know nothing about radios, so I flip the switch from the PA system and tune to the first channel they have listed for emergencies.

"Hello?" I tuck my shoulders in and pray my voice won't crack. If the media gets ahold of this conversation or if a whole room of people is listening, I don't want them to know how terrified I am. My heart is thundering so loud in my ears I can barely hear the static from the radio, but I press on. "This is the Jacksonville to Rockaway Island Ferry. I-Is anyone there?"

They must have been monitoring the channels because a firm voice responds seconds later. "ROF, this is Sheriff Stevens with the Jacksonville Sheriff's Office. Who am I speaking to?"

Thoughts bounce around in my brain like dueling ping-pong balls and it takes a moment for me to pluck my name from the jumble. "T-this is Chloe McKinney."

"Hi, Chloe. Are you okay? Are you hurt?"

I have to press the meat of my palms into my eyes to focus. "I'm okay. I'm not hurt."

"How about everyone else on board? Are there any injuries?"

"T-there was a man who-he—" my voice breaks off. A bubble inflates in my chest, choking the rest of the words.

"The explosion," Sheriff Stevens supplies after a few seconds, his voice gentler. "Was anyone hurt?"

I set my jaw and plant my feet as my breathing slows. "One. I don't believe anyone else is hurt."

"Can you tell me what's going on now? Is there one man, or more?"

"One man, but he's heavily armed. He's...he's put an explosive collar on all of us." Its weight is a constant reminder of its presence. One I don't think I'll ever forget.

"I'm sorry." His voice is tinny from the small speakers. "Can you say that again?"

I glance backward to make sure the man hasn't come up

the stairs behind me and then hunch over the radio now cupped in both my hands. "He has each one of us strapped with explosives. If we get off the boat, like that man did, he sets it off. If we try to hurt him, he sets it off."

He curses under his breath. It's so slight, I don't think he knows I can hear it, but with my ears straining, it's hard for me to miss. "Has he made any demands?"

My tongue darts out to wet my dry lips and I wish for a glass of ice-cold water. "Just that he wants to speak to someone named Gabriel Rossi."

There's a pregnant pause. "I'm sorry, say again?"

I raise my voice and hope the man below can't hear me. "Gabriel Rossi." I hope he can't hear the frantic sound of my breathing over the line. "That's all he said."

"Is he there?" In the background people are yelling and Stevens quiets them with a sharp whistle. "Can you put him on to speak with our negotiators?"

I shake my head before I remember he can't see me. "He said he doesn't want to speak to anyone but Mr. Rossi."

The thud of a boot against steps causes my heart to leap into my throat, so I say the next part in a rush. "Tell your man who just came on board to be careful. This guy is completely serious."

"What did you say?" I hear from the radio as the gunman's head appears at the stairs.

CHAPTER SIX

GABRIEL

THE HOSTAGES down below are huddled together in small groups, head's bowed and arms wrapped around each other. They take no notice when I climb up the back along the rope and peer around the railing. They're too busy listening to the man with the radio dictating rules.

But the woman at the wheel isn't.

On one glance toward the front and her pale, overwrought face finds mine. Her mouth gapes open and her wide eyes flicker toward the man brandishing a gun.

I don't move—I can't. Any quick movements might draw the eyes of any hostage and throw down a storm of unneeded and unnecessary attention. I've already lost one life today; I don't want to risk any more. She looks away for a second and I heft myself up the rest of the way and duck behind the first car.

Aches and pains make themselves known as I crouch behind an old beat up truck with chipped red paint, but push those to the back of my mind.

All of my gear sunk to the bottom of the ocean. I'm unarmed and I'm surrounded by who knows how many explosives ready to go off at the whim of a psychopath.

I'd like to chance looking in each of the cars for a through-and-through American with a glove box stuffed with a semi-automatic, but each one I try is locked.

Threads of conversation carry over the air. From a rough count, I estimate a couple dozen hostages on this floor. Maybe a captain and an attendant up top, plus my girl and their captor.

Despite their outrage, those on this floor keep themselves contained. The show of force the low-life was no doubt counting on with the explosion, is as effective at corralling these people as the bombs strapped to their bodies.

His reminders over the intercom don't hurt, either.

From my vantage point behind a rusted sedan, I can see through one roundish window into the main seating area on the first floor of the ferry. No one else seems to be hurt, but there are plenty crying hysterically and a few who look like they're about to hurl all over the floor.

The stairs leading up to the top, where the woman and captor are, run through the right side of the room, in full few of the rest of the hostages. Walking right out in front of them may do more harm than good, so the stairs are out.

I inch around a couple more cars until I reach the front

railing. The ramp drops off directly in front of me and to my right is a chained off area that will almost guarantee a dip back in the ocean, but it's the only way for me to climb up to listen in on what the bastard's saying.

The deck hangs out over the water so I climb up the railing and feel around for a foothold above me. My fingers clamp down on a notch of wood about an inch thick. It's not much, but it will have to do.

Setting my jaw, I pull myself up by sheer strength of will, my biceps and shoulders burning with the effort. Above me is a rung for the second story railing and I swing one hand up to grasp it, but sweat slicking my palm weakens my grip and I damn near fall right back into the water below.

A growl tears its way through my chest and I surge upward, wrapping my hand around the rail and pulling myself up. I reach my other hand to the next one and keep going until I put a foot on the floor to boost myself the rest of the way over.

There's no opening in the rail on this side, but there is one on the other. I can't stand up here and vault over the rail, because the windows are about waist high, and I don't want to announce my presence before I've had a chance to see what this guy wants.

I inch my way around to the other side, making sure to shore my hands and footing with each step. It's an arduous process, but there's no room for error

With each step it gets easier to hear the goings-on inside the cabin. I sag against the railing when the woman at the wheel comes into sight. Her eyes are bright and glossy with unshed tears. She flinches and shrinks away and I get my first good look at the gunman.

He's about six-foot tall with a trim build. Over his black shirt and nondescript cargo pants are straps wrapping around his shoulders. Two handguns dangle from the holsters. He's older than I expected, maybe forty or forty-five, but his beard and mustache are threaded with gray.

They're speaking too low for me to hear and whatever the man says to her leaves her gaping after him until she collects herself. She rouses the emergency line and speaks with whoever is in charge. If not a hostage negotiator at this point, then certainly Sheriff Stevens.

Then I catch my name from her lips and I nearly release my hold on the railing and fall back into the water.

The fuck?

It scatters the bits of my drive and focus into the wind. Mind racing, breathing labored, it's impossible for me to gather them back up. They explode in a million directions, like shrapnel from an anti-personnel mine in the thick heat of an Afghani desert.

An indeterminable amount of time passes before I can control my breathing, organize my thoughts. I manage to tune back into the conversation, but the feedback is too low for me to hear from my position, so I use the opportunity to climb the rest of the way over the rail and crawl through the shadows to a dark corner by the door where he can't see me.

I give myself a short window to do a little recon before I

burst in. I chance peering around the corner and find the captain bound and gagged in a corner. The woman's low voice fills the room as she speaks to Stevens on the other end. As if drawn by it, I almost take a step inside, but a sound to my left brings me to my senses.

The gunman steps into the room, his hands on his hips, the guns poised at his waist. The woman's eyes flick down to them and then back out the window. "Did you tell them?"

She purses her lips, her eyes pressing together before she answers. "Yes."

His impatient snort causes her to jerk, her arms flaring out like an out-of-control marionette. "Well, are they going to get him?" He leans a hip on the counter next to her and crosses his arms over his chest. When she doesn't answer right away, he pounds a fist against the countertop and she stumbles backward.

Frustration is good for me—it may cause him to make a mistake, but it's also dangerous because it makes him unpredictable. Unpredictable men with weapons are worse than unpredictable women.

"Answer now, pretty bird, before I really get irritated."

"I believe so, yes." She keeps her eyes downcast and her fists coiled tight, the nails digging into her palms, but her response is steady.

Good girl.

His boots scrape against the metal floor and then I hear her swift, pained inhale. I'm close enough now I can hear his next threatening words. People may doubt the presence of evil in this world, but having seen it, and hearing this guy now, there's no doubt in my mind it exists.

Her eyes bulge as he jerks her around and pins her against the edge of the counter. She trembles, but her eyes flash in defiance. "You know if it weren't for you, there'd only be one person on this boat with a bomb strapped to their throat, but because you had to play hero, you've put every person in danger." I risk looking around the corner and find her dangling from his hold, the tips of her toes scratching the floor as he pins the air. She scrabbles against him, her nails clawing at his arm, but he doesn't relent. "Now you will radio those shitheads again and let them know I will execute one hostage every thirty minutes until I speak to him."

His hand tenses in her hair and she squeaks. Then she says, "I thought you said no one would get hurt?"

"I guess it'll be up to you, pretty bird," he replies, then releases his hold.

His tone and his threats make me gnash my teeth. I want to charge in there and expose my position, but my indecision costs me and his footsteps recede back down the stairs.

She starts to open up the radio again and then she stops. The pause draws my attention and I glance through the murky windowpane and find her eyes on me again.

"Please help," she mouths. If I weren't already determined to save her those words would have torn through any resistance.

With one last glance toward the stairwell, I enter the room. Her eyes widen when she realizes I'm almost a foot taller than her. Tension runs through her tight shoulders and pursed lips and I don't want to frighten her more than she already is, so I hold my hands up in surrender.

"Don't be afraid," I say. "My name is Gabriel Rossi. Gabe. I'm here to do whatever I can to help you."

At first I think she doesn't hear me, so I repeat my name in a calm and even tone. I even take a step closer, keeping my hands visible. She doesn't move and her expression is frozen. Worried she may be going into shock, I put a hand on hers, but she snatches back, life blazing into her cheeks with a pink flush.

"Help me?" she screeches. "Help me?" She wedges her fingers underneath the collar and gives it a yank. "You call this *helping* me?"

I frown, but ignore her scathing statement and scan the room. "How long do we have until he comes back?"

"I don't know, I'm not his secretary." Then she pinches her nose between her fingers. "I'm sorry. I don't mean it. I'm just," she heaves a sigh and waves around her free arm, "under a lot of stress."

I put a big hand on her shoulder and try to ignore the warmth of her skin. Her arm drops to her sides and she hides a tremulous smile.

"Now," I say, my mouth firming into a line, my eyes narrowing into slits, "did he say when he will be back?"

"He didn't say," the woman tells me, her eyes flickering back and forth between me and the stairwell.

"Okay, it's okay," I tell her. "What's your name?"

"Chloe," she says. "Chloe McKinney."

I take her shaking hands in mine to steady them. I keep my eyes on hers, try to exude a manner of calm so I don't agitate her even more. "Nice to meet you, Chloe," I say. "The little girl you saved was my daughter, Emily. She and her mother wanted me to tell you thanks for saving her."

Chloe does a double take. "She's your daughter?"

"She was on her way to see me."

"Is she okay? Her mom?"

I squeeze her arms. "They're both fine, just fine. Thanks to you."

She struggles to find the right words, then says, "Good... good. I'm glad they made it out safely. You have a beautiful little girl."

"Thank you." She looks away and I tip her head back with a hand. "I'm gonna get you out of this."

Her head drops forward and then she looks back up. "I sure hope so."

When I feel she's steady, I back off, giving her some space, and get back to business. I do a cursory check of the room to make sure there aren't any surprises. I don't expect him to have another wad of explosives here—I haven't ruled out the possibility elsewhere—but I anticipate finding at least a cache of weapons. Men who pull off maneuvers like this are always well prepared.

I check behind the dash, in crevices, under seat cushions and strike gold in the mini refrigerator, of all places. There I find an MP-5 9mm submachine gun and a slew of handguns crammed into the interior. The contents, including the shelving, had been removed to make room.

I don't move the guns, don't want to risk tipping him off to my location before I'm ready. The fridge makes the slightest creaking sound as I close the door.

"So what's the plan?" she asks, her husky voice a whisper.

"Don't get dead," I tell her.

On top of the fridge I find a box filled with the bomb collars and miscellaneous parts. I find additional locks, but no key.

If he's smart, and I suspect he is, he'll keep the only copy of the key to unlock the collars on his person at all times.

"What are you doing?" she asks from behind me.

I replace the pieces back in their original spots with care. "Making sure there aren't any surprises."

"Not a fan, huh?"

"Not when it comes to my life, no." I peer through cabinet doors and continue my search, making sure to keep from disturbing the snoring captain. "Staying in the hospital just pisses me off."

"Do you end up in the hospital often?" she asks.

I glance over from my inspection of the radio. The smile teasing at her lips makes the response to her question dry up right in my throat.

She raises her eyebrows. "Well?" Her voice is colored with repressed laughter.

For the slightest moment, I wish we'd met under different circumstances. I wish there were a different reason she was smiling and laughing at me. If we were anywhere else, she'd be a woman I'd like to get to know—both in the sheets and out of them.

Because my eyes are still on her smiling mouth, I notice when the smile melts from her lips and then from her gaze. Giving myself a shake, I clear my throat. "More than I like," I say in answer to her earlier question.

She turns away to hide her reaction, but I see her widening eyes and firm lips in response to my frigid tone. Her shoulders stiffen and she straightens, losing what little rapport we shared. I turn away while she does, even though I want to do the opposite. It's better for the both of us if I don't encourage any connection.

I conclude my search of the cabin while the silence between us grows, then I tell her, "We don't have much time before he gets back. I will radio my man on shore for an update and see what we can do about getting everyone out of here without getting them killed."

She nods, but keeps her mouth shut and her attention on the water in front of her.

I punch the buttons on the radio with more force than necessary. Dead air greets my response for a few strained heartbeats.

Then Tyler's sarcastic and reassuring, voice says, "I'm glad you didn't get yourself killed, punk."

My shoulders slump and I slouch into the dash with my head leaning onto my hand. When I speak, my voice is as soft as it can be and still be heard over the scratchy radio connection. "Damn good to hear your voice, old man," I tell Tyler.

His chuckle is familiar and welcome. "Bit of a clusterfuck you've gotten yourself into," he says.

"Well, you know how I attract trouble."

"Crazy son-of-a-bitch," he mutters. "You're gonna have hell to pay if you do get back here in one piece. Stevens is going on a rampage."

"Tell me something new," I say. "Does he have a plan or are they floundering?"

"They've got a negotiator, but so far no luck connecting with your guy."

"No shit? I heard he won't talk to anyone but me. Any lead on what that's about?"

"None so far, but trust me, I'm working on it. Pissed anyone off lately?"

"Guess we'll find out. But I want to get as many hostages off here before our guy gets trigger happy and I have a feeling he won't be pleased when he finds me here, which will happen sooner or later." I pause while I consider my options. "Think Stevens will go for sending rescue teams to intercept?"

"How do you plan to convince the kidnapper to go for it?"

"He doesn't have to know I'm here...yet. If we could get him to head toward the teams without knowing they'll be there waiting, the element of surprise may work in our favor."

"And if not?"

"If not, I'll offer myself as a bargaining chip."

Chloe, who's been silent during our conversation, gasps

beside me. It's a small sound and if the wheelhouse wasn't so quiet because we are trying not to draw any attention to ourselves, I wouldn't have heard it. But since I do, since I can't help but notice her presence so close, I turn to look at her.

She's working her lip with her teeth. The bottom one is blood-red from constant attention. I don't think she realizes it, but she's shaking her head in barely noticeable twitches.

To Tyler, I say, "If you can convince Stevens to go along with it, have them meet us." I rattle off a location not far from where we are.

"I'll do what I can," Tyler says. "You be smart. Selene will skin me alive if something happens to you."

"I will," I say. And I hope I'm right.

I hang up the handset and turn my attention to Chloe, whose hands are now knotted around the wheel.

Before I can give her directions, she says, "Where do I need to go?"

The determined pull of her mouth almost makes me smile. Almost.

"We want to get him as close to the coast as possible. Say whatever you have to say to convince him."

Then she flattens me when she says, "What if I suggest the police need us closer due to the storm and radio signal?"

I nod. "Yeah. Yeah, that'll work."

She looks away, then back at me. "What about...what about you?"

My first instinct is offer comfort, which I neither have the time or the ability to do at this point, so I try for honesty instead.

"I'll keep low until we meet with the rescue team."

"And if he doesn't let the hostages go? You'll give yourself up to him? This isn't a game."

"Trust me," I tell her as I back through the door. "If it was a game, I'd be playing to win."

CHLOE

I've never known what a privileged life I lead until one choice threatened to take it all away. Slices of memories race before my eyes as I stare, unseeing, through the window in front of me.

My parents, who've lived on opposite sides of Florida since their divorce, love me—in their own off-handed sort of way. My two sisters fought each other—and me—the entire time we were caged under the same roof. Since we all moved out and moved on with our own lives and worries and ambitions, we've never kept the tight bond I've seen most other families cultivate. But I love the lot of them. Much as I've complained over the years, I'd give anything to see all of them one more time.

As the ancient clock affixed to the wall next to me ticks off the passing time with maddening regularity, I remember each of their faces. My mother, whose dark hair has recently become threaded with gray. The last time I saw her was during her Christmas visit and we stood in the aisle in the middle of the drugstore as she contemplated whether or not to buy hair colorant. After a heated debate about two brands of the exact same shade of blackish-brown, she'd decided to get it done at a salon instead.

At the time, it made me want to throw a tantrum like a five-year-old right in the middle of the store, but now, I'd repeat that moment a million times over.

The same goes for any of the countless, meaningless fights with my sisters. They take after my mom when it comes to looks. Impish little faces and straight falls of identical black-brown hair. Two and three years younger than me, they always banded together against me, leaving me the odd man out.

I take after my father and I can see him in my reflection in the window. Sharper, stronger features. A tough chin and full, expressive mouth. Unlike my sisters, my hair doesn't know which shade it wants to be. It's predominantly brown, but in the right light it takes on an auburn hue.

I picture his face as I stare at my own and I can hear him lecturing me about checking my oil or hurricane-proofing my apartment. He likes to show his affection by doling out maintenance advice and Mr. Fix-It services. When my ex broke up with me, he offered to caulk my tub. If I get out of this mess, I bet he'll be willing to build me a house from the ground up.

A flash of white in the window catches my attention and I realize I'm smiling at the thought. My reflection makes a hysterical giggle bubble up in my throat and threaten to burst free.

Clearly, I'm not cut out for this kind of stress.

The urge to laugh fades and the icy weight of terror returns to lodge in my stomach. Long after this night ends, if it ever does, the sound of boots coming up the stairs will send a shot of fear down my spine. I'll never be able to hear that sound and not think of this man walking up behind me, gun at the ready.

His face appears in the window beside my own. For a moment he doesn't say a word. He peers out into the blackness like he can see things in the shadows and dark I can't.

After a tense silence, he says, "Did you do as I asked?"

I release my bottom lip from between my teeth. "Yes, they said he's on the way, but we're starting to get out of range of their radios. If you want to speak to Gabriel, we'll have to angle back toward the coast."

I suck in a long, slow breath to calm my rambling, then peek at him next to me to gauge his response. He'll either flip his shit and blow me to bits, or he'll demand they come closer.

The muscles in his strong, jutting jaw clench and release, then he says, "Idiots. Would lose their heads if they didn't have a fucking map to find them. Fine, yeah, follow their heading and then let me know when they have Rossi on the radio."

Behind us the captain is coming to with a loud groan followed by a series of grunts. I flick a look between the both of them, then take the plunge.

"Um," I start, "Mr....?"

"Call me Jones," he says as he turns to face me with furrowed brows.

"Mr. Jones," I repeat, then glance toward the groaning captain. "Should I help him?" I jerk my head toward the man. He's got his eyes open and is trying to blink away the blood dripping down his forehead.

Jones scoffs and turns from him. "Leave him. He'll live."

I purse my lips in an effort to keep my retort back and focus on readjusting our direction toward the Florida coast-line. It shouldn't take long, but I know the decisions we make in the next few minutes risk all our lives.

With a furtive glance at Mr. Jones, I say, "We should hear something from them in the next few minutes."

He says nothing in return, but he does toy with a paper-clip on the dash and switch his weight from his left foot to his right, and then back again. His gaze darts between the radio and the invisible line of the coast in the distance.

My breath comes out in little pants and I have to wipe my clammy hands on my clothes to keep them from slipping on the steering wheel. The necklace slips and slides on my throat, the weight listing with the movement of the heavy lock from side to side. I desperately want to clear my throat, but I don't dare draw any more attention to myself.

Finally, when I fear I may vomit or faint, or a combination of the two, I spot the faint bluish-green line of land to our right. The knot inside my stomach loosens and I take a deep, though not calming, breath.

Then, the ferry gives a great shudder and jerks to a stop. I find myself sprawled over the dash in front of me, my nose and lip throbbing viciously from the impact. I straighten and touch a hand to the tender flesh. My fingers come away stained red with blood.

I blink my eyes rapidly to get my blurry vision to clear, then I realize the reason why it's hard to see is because someone's shining a bright spotlight on the front of the ferry.

"This is the Jacksonville's Sheriff's Office. We'd like to speak with the individual in charge."

Mr. Jones turns and my knees wobble. The gun is pressed to my temple before I can offer an explanation. I don't get the chance to faint like I want to before he's grabbing me up with his free hand, his grip bruising the flesh on my wrist, and pulling me in front of him as a human shield. In mere seconds I have not only one, but three guns aimed at me.

Two officers flank the Coast Guard vessel in front of the now stationary ferry. Another two man a huge spotlight. Yet another has a megaphone.

"I want to speak to Gabriel Rossi," Jones shouts before they have a chance to say another word. "Right now or I'll start executing hostages."

"We're working on it," the man with the megaphone says. "But as a show of faith, why don't you offer to let some of those innocent people go? It'll grease the wheels with the brass."

The muzzle of the gun bites into my head. I swear I can almost feel it drilling into my skull. Sweat, or blood, drips down my cheek and salts my lips. I don't dare move to wipe it away.

His responding laugh is bitter and hollow in my ear. "You're not gettin' shit until I get what I want." Jones shuffles behind me as he checks his watch. "Running out of time, boss. Got five minutes before I execute the first hostage."

Controlled chaos explodes on the other boat. Officers converse over the radios, others rush back and forth with materials, setting up God-only-knows what kinds of gadgets and weapons. My vision blurs and I blink rapidly. I will not cry. I may not see tomorrow morning, but I won't let this bastard see me cry.

Picturing Gabe's competent and steady hands as he searched the cabin, his reassuring voice, his self-assurance, allows my breathing and my thoughts slow. As if he can sense my inner calm, Jones' arms vice around me, squeezing what little air remains out of my lungs, his will trying to dominate my own.

"They won't save you," he says in my ear. "No one can save you."

"You're wrong," I tell him. His arm tightens and I gasp helplessly for air against his grip.

"I guess we'll find out, won't we?"

"You don't expect to get out of this alive, do you?" I wheeze. I can only draw in pants of air at this point and white spots fill my vision. "The entire police department is waiting for you. They've probably mobilized the Coast Guard, contacted the F.B.I. You've already killed one person. If you're aiming for a police-assisted suicide you're on the right track."

"You have no idea what I expect to get out of this." His eyes are on the officers on the other boat, but he trembles behind me and I know I've struck a chord.

"A lot of dead bodies?" I hazard.

"Next one will be yours if you don't shut your trap," he growls.

"If that were the case you would have killed me a long time ago. Waving a gun in my face is starting to get a little old."

"Oh, I've got more planned for you, pretty bird. Just you wait."

"Fuck you."

Jones twists and shoves me to the ground with one powerful hand in between my shoulder blades. My knees and palms take the brunt of the damage, as the thin carpeting covering the floor doesn't provide much cushion. It doesn't crack, but my right wrist gives under the impact and I crumple with a shout of pain.

I rest my weight on my left arm as I get up to my knees. I don't have time for theatrics, can't allow myself the opportunity to give in to the pain radiating up my arm. Staying curled up in the fetal position on the ground isn't an option. Cradling my injured arm close to my chest, I clamber to unsteady feet.

My eyes strain to the bench that opens to storage where I know Gabe lies in wait. I send mental signals I know he can't hear for him not to jump out yet.

I nearly let the threatening laughter spill over my lips, but manage to hold it back as I hear the gun cock startlingly close to my head. A person shouldn't be this comfortable with death so close, but the constant adrenaline rush has overwhelmed my common sense—along with any other emotions.

Jones grabs my arm with a bruising grip and the gun presses intimately underneath my jaw, a lethal kiss. He shoves me again, pushing me toward the stairs. Pale faces shine up at me, blurring together as he knocks me forward. I stumble and take hold of the railing before I take the plunge down the stairs, momentarily forgetting my injured arm. A scream threatens to rip from my throat, but I suck it back.

"Pick one," he says. "Since you got rid of the girl, it'll be up to you who dies tonight."

It would be easier if he'd just shoot me.

Picking up my feet is almost impossible. I have the sudden, irrational fear if I were to fall overboard they would turn into concrete blocks and sink me down to the bottom of the ocean. My thighs strain with the effort it takes to pick up one foot and place it on the next step.

It's a different world on the first floor. The resentful looks and anger are ravaged by fear. All around me I see the whites of terrified eyes. For each move I make toward them, they take a collective step backward, like I'm the personification of death and they know it's catching.

Sweat drips down my forehead despite the cold that wracks my body. I wipe it away with an impatient hand and stare at the faces of the people I'm supposed to sacrifice, but all I can see is the face of Gabe's little girl.

"Time's up," Jones says.

I turn back to face him and climb back up the stairs before I have time to change my mind.

Jones stares at me with a half-smile pulling on his monstrous lips. "Well?"

"Me."

He stares, then jerks his gun at me. "Playing the martyr again are we?"

"You can't make me choose," I say. "If you want to kill someone, you're going to have to kill me."

Jones looks at me, then at the boat full of cops and before I can read his actions, he pivots, strides to the stairs, and shoots a young woman, who can't be more than nineteen, in the center of her forehead. She goes down, her face frozen in a gasp of eternal fear. The only evidence of her demise is a small dark circle and a thin trail of blood on her brow.

When time speeds back up, I find myself cowering on the floor, my hands covering my head in an instinctual response. Disoriented, I shake my head to clear it of the echo from the gunshot and reach out for something, anything to hold onto. I grip a rail and only realize I used my strained arm when it starts throbbing. Cradling it, I take automatic steps away from the sight of the dead woman and nearly trip over Gabe as he storms down the stairs behind me.

"Rossi." If it weren't for the twinge of movement at his

brows and the microcosm of a frown around his lips, I wouldn't have caught Jones' surprise at Gabe's appearance.

Gabe moves in front of me, his broad shoulders blocking the horrific sight from view. Without thinking, I inch closer and burrow my face into the space between his shoulder blades. For a fleeting second, his left hand finds mine. He clasps it, squeezes, and steps forward.

"I'll talk to you under one condition."

Jones lips twitch for a second. "It doesn't seem like you're in the position for negotiations."

Gabe climbs out of the bench, his hands still raised in front of him. "You're the one who wanted to talk so badly. If you want to talk, then let's do it. Let these people go and we can gab as long as you fuckin' please."

"And get rid of my only bargaining chip?" Jones questions.

"I'll stay," I blurt out.

Both men turn and the expressions on their faces couldn't be more different. Jones looks...happy and if that isn't frightening enough, Gabe's entire body is trembling, probably with the effort it takes to restrain him from murdering me himself.

"Let them go," I say, my voice surprisingly steady, "and I'll stay. You'll have two hostages and a ferry to bargain with. You've already got the entire state of Florida's attention, if not the whole country's."

Gabe controls himself long enough to add, "Those are my conditions. Let everyone else go and we'll talk."

Jones considers it for a second. "Get on your knees," he tells Gabe, who shakes his head.

"I'm not doing shit until those people are safe."

"So we have two martyrs on board," Jones says. In a flash faster than I'd expect from an older man, he pummels Gabe over the head with the butt of the gun and then he turns. "Get on your knees and don't move."

I drop next to Gabe until Jones disappears down the stairs. His chest is lifting, barely, and when I shake him he groans.

"Oh, thank God," I whisper. For a tense second, I thought he was dead, too. I don't dare move him, but I move to his side, unsure of what to do to help him. "Gabe?" I whisper.

My hands run along his face as he fights unconsciousness, memorizing the features I was too frightened to pay attention to the first time I saw him. My fingers map the defined line of his square jaw covered in thick, raspy stubble. They travel over his chapped lips and hollow cheeks to his heavy brow and closed lids. Beneath my fingertips his eyes flutter and I have to wipe away a tear as it streaks from my own. His hair is still damp from the ocean and I frown when my hands come away soaked in red.

With a yelp, I take off my cardigan and hold it up to his forehead to soak up the blood oozing from the gash. I flash to the memory of the girl falling not minutes before and I'm overcome with a mindless panic. I can't be here alone. He can't leave me here alone. I'll be okay as long as he's here.

"Gabe?" His name breaks as a sob nearly tears its way out of my throat.

My eyes flutter closed when he stops groaning. I duck my head, my chin pressing into my chest. The world around me, blockaded behind the numbing effect of adrenaline, comes rushing back, filling my ears with the sound of screams from everyone downstairs, the orders from the sheriff's on the boat, and the stunning silence from Gabe.

I have no illusions about making it off this boat alive. I know the chances are slim, and grow even more desolate with each passing moment and execution, but those odds are easier to face when I have someone to lean on.

A bracing wind helps to clear my thoughts and my eyes snap open to find his staring back at me. Warmth floods my chest and I launch myself at him, not thinking about my arm. He catches me and I whimper as my hand comes in contact with the floor.

With a groan he sits up, still holding me. His warmth combats the chill and I look up, startled to find myself sitting on his lap, surrounded by his arms. The cardigan flutters to my lap and I retrieve it to press against his wound.

He winces and then his hands are on me. They trace my legs and my breath strangles in my throat at his touch. I don't catch it until his fingers probe the tender swollen mass of my wrist. "Are you okay?" He winces and cradles his head, his hands fumbling around mine on the makeshift bandage. "Shit. This wasn't how I planned to spend this weekend."

"Yeah, me neither." He starts to stand, but I stop him with a hand on his arm. "Wait, let's make sure your head isn't still bleeding."

He humors me while I dab at his wound until the flow of blood slows to a trickle. "Diagnosis?"

The cardigan is ruined, nearly soaked through with red, so I toss it under the dash. "I think you'll live."

He eases me off his lap and then gets to his feet. He holds out a hand and I take it. "How's your arm?"

"Hurts like hell, but I'll be okay."

"Whatever happens next just follow my lead, okay?"

I don't have time to answer because Jones reappears with an armful of collars dangling from his wrist. He nods to the boat, spotlights still trained on us. "Make the trade," he says.

CHAPTER SEVEN

GABRIEL

"Didn't I tell you not to get yourself dead?"

"I'm not dead yet," I tell Tyler over the radio. "Good news, though. Have them move the boat to the back. Jones is gonna let the rest of the hostages off."

"How the hell did you manage that?"

I ignore the question and say, "He took off the explosives so Stevens needs to move his ass before this guy changes his mind."

"They've deployed boats to remove the hostages. You stay there and keep your man calm while we direct them off the ferry."

"I'll do what I can." My voice low, I add, "And see if there is anything you can find about former customers I've had or rescue operations involving anyone named Jones. Maybe someone I dealt with during my time in the Corps. I don't know what the hell this sonofabitch wanted with Emily, Ty, but we need to find out. And as soon as you can."

"Jones," Tyler repeats back. "I'm on it, Gabe. I promise."

"How are things on the mainland?"

"Smooth as they can be. Will you and your lady friend be ready to move if our friends over here rock the boat?"

I hiss out a string of curses, but don't let my body language communicate anything. "Jesus Christ, Ty, are you *trying* to get me killed."

"Starting to think you're like a cat, Rossi. I'm sure you've got a couple lives left to spare."

"Try not to use them all in one go," I tell him.

After I hang the radio back on the hook, I press my lips into a line and turn to face him. Chloe stands between us, her whole body trembling. I catch her gaze with my own and communicate my concern with a twitch of my brows. She frowns for a second and then she nods. With my hands loose, unassuming and unthreatening by my sides, I take a tentative step toward them both.

Jones jerks his gun and twitches it toward the bench. "No fast movements," he says. "You take a seat there and keep your hands where I can see them."

I do as he says and I keep him in my eyesight the whole time. When I'm sitting with my hands resting on my thighs, Jones shoves Chloe across the room and I catch her just before she goes down on her injured wrist. She doesn't make a sound, but what little color remaining in her face drains away. I try to help her up, but she gives her head a little shake and stands on her own. By the time she collapses in the seat next to me, her lips white. Her body is as taut as a bowstring, but she jerks her chin up and maintains eye contact with Jones.

The stubborn jut of her chin almost makes me grin. She may appear to be an angel, but she's got the spirit of a warrior.

"You two stay right here while they unload the cargo from below," Jones is saying when I turn back to face him. "Put out your hands."

I won't gain anything from arguing with him, so I do as he says, even though it makes my skin crawl to be at his mercy. He zip-ties Chloe's wrists in front of her first and I don't miss the wince when he jostles her injured wrist. It's already turning colors and I'm worried it may be broken instead of just strained.

A chilling grin pulls at Jones' lips by the time he finishes with her and gets to me. First is the collar around my neck followed by restraining my wrists. He's humming and all the earlier tension that seemed to grip him about the surprise visit from the sheriffs is gone. In fact, he seems...happy? For someone with no less than ten weapons trained on him this very moment, he's too relaxed. Especially considering we outwitted him and he's cornered, giving up the one bargaining chip he had. Three hostages—including the captain—is nothing compared to the dozens he's voluntarily giving up.

Something about it nags at me.

I know there's an ulterior motive at play. A man doesn't just hijack a boat with this many hostages on a whim and then relinquish them at the first chance. Which means either he has what, or in this case who, he wants, and he no longer needs those hostages, or he has something else planned for us.

It's pitch black out, but the spotlights from the Coast Guard's boat are trained on the area where they're preparing to unload the small crowd of people. They've situated a makeshift ramp and are helping everyone off one by one, a few uniformed officers guiding them along the wobbly plank.

If I were him, I'd have contingency plans. He has to know a boat isn't the most secure place. He has to know being ambushed by the cops was an option. Since he's got me, they're no longer important.

And then it hits and before I can second guess myself, my brain goes into auto-pilot and I move.

Jones has his attention on the people unloading, no doubt to calculate his next move, so he doesn't see me dive for the throttle. I engage it with my bound hands, but it does the job. The ferry jerks forward, throwing me to the ground. The people down below squawk and I hear their distressed screams before they are swallowed by the ocean.

All this happens in a manner of seconds, but it's enough to wipe the cheerful expression off the bastard's face and it gives me some level of satisfaction.

Then another explosion rents the air and throws us both to the ground. The boat shudders and for a moment I'm terrified we're going down, then it stabilizes and sputters forward. I've seen a lot of shit in my life, but for a few seconds, I can't bear to look up. The fear of seeing what horrifying thing is waiting for me paralyzes my thoughts.

"Gabe," comes a desperate whisper. "Gabe!"

I roll over to my back with a groan and consider the view. "We have to stop meeting like this," I tell the two of her.

She slaps at me with her bound hands and I grab it, which jars my throbbing head. "Why would you do that?" she screeches. "Do you have a death wish?"

I think about it for a second, then I say, "No, I don't think so."

She grabs a pair of scissors after searching the dash drawers and releases both of our bound hands. My head spins as she helps me to my feet. Mayhem greets me, and it takes a few minutes for my brain to decipher what my eyes are seeing. The tail of the boat is engulfed in smoke and the scent of singed plastic and hot metal. A cacophony of shouts pepper the air and then there's a rapid-fire *pop-pop-pop* from an automatic weapon.

Chloe wedges her shoulder under my arm to help me to my feet. Still reeling from the rush of adrenaline, I wrap an arm around her waist and we both go back down to the ground at the first sound of gunfire.

I shield her body with my own, tucking her face into my neck and caging her with both of my arms. "Don't move."

Her body vibrates with fear, but when I scan her expression, there's fire in her eyes. "Was that him?" She strains against me to get a better view of the lower deck. "Did they get him?"

"I don't know, but I have a feeling I'm not that lucky."

"Oh, you're definitely not lucky today," Jones says from behind us.

CHLOE

Above me, Gabe's body becomes one long, hard line of hate. My blood is pumping and my reflexes are all heightened so when I feel the six feet of male pressed against me from top to bottom, heat, oblivious to the situation, washes over me.

His glare is lethal and the hand on my shoulder contracts with bruising strength. I don't think he knows he's doing it and I don't dare interrupt their epic stare-down. If they'd been in the Wild West, guns would be drawn.

Jones doesn't point the angry-looking rifle he has slung from his shoulder at us, but I feel it watching me as he strides across the room to the controls. He sets it on top of the dash and I have a hard time turning away from it to see what his hands are doing.

"First chance I get, I will get you off of here," Gabe says in a half-whisper. His breath tickles my ear and I shiver against him.

I pray he doesn't feel it. In fact, I even close my eyes for the barest half-second. But when I open them, I see his slightly widened and want to throw myself overboard.

Then he glances down my body, his grip releasing, and slightly pats me down with his free hand. A moan nearly tears itself from my throat.

I bat his hands away and nearly head-butt him when I sit

up. All I can think is I need to get away. "I'm fine," I say, more sharply than I intend. My butt scrapes against the rough carpeting as I put some much-needed space between us. "No need to manhandle me."

Gabe squints at me, like I'm a problem he can't quite figure out, but I turn a wary eye to Mr. Jones, who's taken ahold of the wheel and seems to have forgotten us. While he's distracted, I get to my feet. The air around me is stifling. Tension pours out in waves from both men and I'm stuck right in the middle.

Jones has shifted into full throttle and the cumbersome ferry plows through the waves like they're nothing. We're going faster than I ever expected this thing to go—and we're headed straight for emptiness.

When we're far enough away the rescue boat is but a blip in the distance, he slows us down until he finally brings the ferry to a stop. It couldn't have taken more than a few minutes, but in the middle of nowhere, it feels like we've traveled across galaxies instead of just a couple miles. The adrenaline's worn off and I'm scraped raw inside. If I do make it out of here, I'm terrified of what, if anything, will be left of me.

Gabe is shooting me furtive glances from where he leans against the wall to my opposite. Remembering all too well the way he felt against me, and hating myself for even thinking of it for a moment, I try my best to keep my eyes downcast.

I feel very alone. I press a hand to my knotted middle as if I can contain the ballooning fear inside of me. When it feels as though a scream—or my heart itself—may burst right out of my chest, I bite down on a knuckle. An indeterminable amount of time passes as I try to control the raging tempest inside of me.

All I can think about is the explosion. The injured passengers. Was there anything I could have done to save them? If I hadn't jumped in front of the little girl, would more lives be spared? Was the blood of those who died today on my hands? There were kids amongst those survivors. Did they make it to safety in time?

The thought spurs me to my feet and I pace in tight circles, growing increasingly blind to my surroundings as panic overwhelms me like a rogue wave. I rake my hands through my hair and my fingers snag on snarls. Chunks come away as I try to wrest my hands free.

A heavy weight blankets my shoulders until warmth from the body behind me washes away the icy shroud. "You're okay," he says. There's an indefinite pause as my mind jerks back from the brink of sanity and then I recognize his hold around me. When I tune back in, I hear his calm, steady voice repeating, "You're okay. I've got you," in a soothing refrain.

My knuckles are white where my fists clench around his forearms. "I'm sorry," I whisper so only he can hear. "I just need a minute."

His hold never falters. "I'm not goin' anywhere," he says. "Take all the time you need."

When I'm sure I won't fall apart, I ease myself out of the circle of his arms. With a rueful smile in his general direction,

I straighten my clothes, smooth back my hair, and take a few deep, calming breaths.

I open my mouth to apologize, but he waves it away. "Don't worry about it," he says. "We all have to fall apart every now and then."

His words wring a surprised laugh from me. "I'll remind you of that when this is over."

We both turn toward the sound of footsteps. Before Jones can reach us, Gabe says in a low voice, "You can remind me at dinner when this is over."

There isn't any time to respond because Jones is grabbing me roughly by my uninjured arm and forcing me to kneel in the middle of the room. Much as I've been thrown around in the past few hours, I should be used to it.

I want to turn around. I want to be able to see my fate—if the situation devolves to that. I don't want to die a coward. But at the same time, I'm terrified of what I'm going to find.

"Sit down," I hear Jones say to Gabe. I don't need to look up after all, because I can hear the tell-tale click of the gun pointed in my direction.

From the corner of my eye, I see Gabe's bare feet* come into view. It strikes me as a particularly vulnerable part of a man and this one specifically. He seemed so formidable charging in here like he was the proverbial knight-in-shining-armor.

Only this knight has no armor to stand between him and the path of a bullet.

"Whatever you want, you want it from me, so deal with

me," Gabe says. My body is once again wracked with shivers and it yearns for the warmth emanating from his proximity.

"Oh, I am dealing with you," Jones replies. "Apparently, a show of force is the only language you understand."

"Then leave her out of it."

Jones chuckles and it only increases my trembling. "I think this will be a whole lot easier if you have the proper motivation." There's the rustle of clothes, the whisper of his cotton shirt brushing against his body. "Sit down over there while we have our conversation. If you play by the rules, then it will be a civilized one."

Gabe does as Jones instructs and I watch his feet recede while I scan what little I can see of the room from my kneeling position.

Jones pulls up a chair next to me and the gun comes into my line of vision, freezing the breath right in my chest.

"Look at me," Gabe says and my eyes find him. "Whatever happens, you keep your eyes on me, okay, honey?"

"Don't talk to her." Jones moves in Gabe's line of vision.

Gabe holds my eyes defiantly for a few long seconds until I nod, then he glances back to Jones. "What would you like to talk about?" he asks in an even voice.

"You must be happy," Jones says and his congenial tone makes me want to gag. He sounds *pleased* with himself.

Gabe barely even bats an eye. Because yes, I'm not going to take my eyes off of him until we have the reassuring solidity of land beneath our feet. "What should I be happy about?"

He must be damn good at whatever job he has. I don't

think I heard him say exactly. From his ease in this high stakes debacle, it has to be something with a lot of stress because he's cool under all the pressure.

At least one of us seems to be.

"You think you've already won," Jones says. His legs cross in my line of vision. Just passed where the two of them are sitting, I can see the captain's chest rising and falling in his peaceful slumber, the lucky bastard.

"Hard to win a game I don't even know I'm playing," Gabe replies evenly.

"Don't be stupid, Gabriel. We both know you're smarter than that."

"Since you seem to know so much, why don't you explain to me what exactly you want from me."

"I want you to remember."

A furrow between Gabe's brows is the only outward reaction he has to Jones's cryptic statement. "I'll do whatever you want, remember whatever the hell you want," Gabe says and he jerks his chin at me, "as long as you let Chloe go."

"Ohhh. It's Chloe now, is it? Getting friendly, are we?"

Gabe grits his teeth. "She doesn't have anything to do with this."

Jones crosses a leg nonchalantly. "She volunteered for the position." He waves the subject of me away like a gnat. "Besides, you'll be most uncooperative if I give away my leverage. So long as you answer my questions honestly, she'll be completely safe."

"Like those hostages were safe?" Gabe asks acidly.

Jones *tsks*. "Now, Gabe, I wasn't the one who lured me into a trap. You didn't think you were going to get away with that little stunt, did you?"

"They were innocent," Gabe says.

"Everyone is innocent. That doesn't mean they're exempt. Innocent people die every day, Mr. Rossi, or are you not aware?"

Gabe's response is silence.

"Now, tell me about yourself, Gabriel."

His nostrils flare. "Are you sure this is how you want to spend your limited time on this Earth?" he asks instead of answering.

Jones chuckles. "No, I imagine I'll spend it watching the life drain from your eyes. Until then, answer the question, or I'll shoot your little damsel here and I won't be picky about where."

CHAPTER EIGHT

GABRIEL

Recognizing the rock and its bitch, the hard place, I relent. "What do you want to know?" I ask.

There's a fanatic gleam in Jones' eyes now. One that tells me whatever fucked up finale he's twisting around in that brain of his will happen—soon. So the best I can do for Chloe and me is stall him for time until the badges on shore can figure out a plan B. One that ends with the two of us alive.

If not, then I need to figure out an end game of my own.

Jones smiles. "Why don't you start with your daughter?"

There's a strangled sound from the captain and all of our eyes go to his limp body. When he doesn't rouse, the attention swings back in my direction.

The question twists itself in my chest like a pissed-off pit of vipers. Jones seems positively beside himself with glee. The maniacal smile that's more of a grimace draws his pale face taut in the moonlight.

When I say nothing, Jones jabs Chloe in the ribs with the muzzle of the gun. He turns and lifts a brow.

I'm not the kind of man who enjoys death. There are some who find a small measure of sick satisfaction when they take a life. A lot of men I've worked with over the years find it a sense of relief when they rid the world of bad men, but I've taken no pleasure in it.

But, for this man, I'd be willing to make an exception.

"Why her?" I ask instead of answering. "Why not just come to me? If you have a problem, you come to me. You don't go after my kid. You don't kill a bunch of people like a toddler on a power trip. Be a man. Confront me."

Jones cocks his head to the side and studies me. It's disconcerting, even to someone like me, having faced war for years on end, to stare into the face of an evil man.

"I'll be asking the questions," he says, after a time. "Yours will be answered. Eventually."

Chloe is as still as a statue, except for her hands. They're clasped behind her back and completely bleached of any color because she's holding them so tightly. Her fingers twitch in their restrained position and it undoes me.

"What do you want to know?" I ask Jones.

The gun eases off of her ribs and he rests his hands on the table. "Her name is Emily, right?" And I know when his face twitches he already knows her name. He'd have to. I offer a fervent prayer of thanks that my baby girl is far, far away from here thanks to Chloe.

"Yes," I say, and my voice sounds like it's being filtered through gravel. I wince and clear my throat. "Yes, her name's Emily." This time, her name is a whisper.

"Do you love your daughter, Gabriel?" Jones asks.

"Of course I do."

"How much do you love her?"

"What kind of question is that?" I ask between gritted teeth. "I love her very much."

Jones just smiles his creepy-ass psychopath smile and labors across the room to the dashboard where he checks the digital GPS. "We're here," he says as he turns back to us. "Don't you move now."

He disappears down the stairs again, his boots thudding heavily in retreat.

"What's he doing now?" Chloe whispers.

I shake my head. "I have no fuckin' idea."

"Any bright ideas?" she asks.

"I'll figure something out," I tell her.

And I hope I'm right.

"That sounds totally promising," she says and startles a laugh out of me.

"Well, I aim to please," I say.

Whatever her response will be is cut off by the horrendous clank of a chain smashing against its metal counterpart, followed by a splash of water.

"Well, wherever we are," she says instead, "we won't be going anywhere."

The boat jerks as the anchor takes hold of the ocean floor.

"We're stranded," I say absently.

"In another time," I hear her respond, "being stranded with you wouldn't be such a bad thing."

"If we get out of this, I have this cottage on the beach. I think you'd like it."

"Are you hitting on me?" she asks softly.

I don't get the chance to answer because Jones appears in the stairwell. I'm going to enjoy kicking his motherfucking ass when I get the opportunity.

Jones sits opposite me. "Now, where were we?"

"Why did you want me here?" I ask plainly. "What do you want?"

"So eager," Jones says. "Very well. I'm here because I'd like to get to know the illustrious Gabriel Rossi better, though from our short acquaintance, I've found you to be pathetically predictable."

"Have you?" I sneer. "And why is that?"

Jones picks at his sleeve with feigned nonchalance. "At first I was concerned her interference completely ruined months of careful planning." He flicks an annoyed glance at Chloe. "Then, to my surprise, you came anyway. I must know, what was your motivation?"

Her gaze is already on me when I peer in her direction. "It was the right thing to do," I say to them both.

Chloe's eyes shutter closed and a wave of pain crosses her face, pinching her brows and lips.

"The right thing to do," Jones says, drawing my attention back to him. "Interesting. Do you consider yourself a good person?"

"No better than any other man," I say.

"How humble," Jones says scathingly. "Is your charitable nature why you volunteer with the Coast Guard?"

"I wouldn't call it charity. I've always loved serving my country."

"Do you enjoy saving lives, Mr. Rossi?" he asks, the smile now gone from his too-wide lips.

"I enjoy being helpful."

"Helpful. Hmm. Do you want to know what I think?"

"I'm sure you're going to tell me."

The squawk from the radio cuts off his answer. Above the sounds of my racing heart, I can hear Tyler's urgent voice. When I scan back at Jones, I find him staring at the unconscious body of the captain.

"Gabe, you there?" Though the connection is terrible and filled with crackling, it's unmistakably Tyler.

Jones smiles, but this time, he seems almost resigned. "Better get that, Rossi. Don't worry, we'll wait." He drops a hand to Chloe's hair and strokes. I don't miss the shiver that wracks her body and I doubt it has anything to do with the wind.

I lurch to my feet and nearly go back down. Guess that explosion knocked my head around a bit more than I thought.

The dash, luckily, isn't too far away, and I catch myself on the edge and manage to stay on my feet.

"Gabe?" crackles the radio.

I fumble with the handheld and hold it up to my mouth. "Tyler, it's Gabe."

"Gabe, good to hear from you after that shit show. Can you talk?"

The radio may be filled with static, but Jones is close enough that he can hear every word Tyler's saying so I glance to him for confirmation. When he nods, I turn back and say into the radio, "Yeah, I can talk. What have you got?"

"There are hundreds of people with the last name Jones," he starts.

"Well, that's helpful."

"So, I went digging. We can assume, from his insistence that he had to have you and no one else, that he's tied to you in some way, so we've had every man on the ground looking into your background for any possible ties."

"I hope you're calling because you found one."

"We damn near didn't. But I knew the name sounded familiar, but it didn't click until I started searching into all the rescue ops for the past five years. There was a woman about a year ago? Her small fishing boat had gotten caught during a squall. We ended up having to call off the search."

I press my fingers into my bleary eyes trying to pull the details from my muddled thoughts. Then it hits me all at once and I nearly stagger backward. Her name had been Sheila Langford-Jones.

Jones. *Jones.* **Jones**.

The color drains from my face and I have to white knuckle the dash to keep from keeling over.

"I remember," I say hoarsely, and I lean heavily against the dash as I turn to face the man whose wife I couldn't save. "I was the one leading the team." By the end, my voice is barely audible.

"You're the reason why I'm all alone, Mr. Rossi," Jones says.

CHLOE

My father was always a stoic man. In fact, I don't think I can even remember ever seeing him cry. As a police officer, he'd seen a lot of horrific things and he was raised to keep those things locked up tight. I never saw him seek my mother out for comfort. He was affectionate, to a point, but not very open. I imagine he was that way because if he ever did open up, all the pain and fear and regret could never be shoved back in and sewn up again.

If he'd ever broken, I imagine he'd bear a striking resemblance to Gabe when he realizes why Jones orchestrated this whole horrific ordeal.

The fight goes out of him and he slumps against the console behind him. The string keeping his spine straight snaps and he crumples and his hands cover his eyes as though he can blot out the images running across his brain.

I itch to cross the room and offer him something, anything,

to comfort him, but Jones towers by my side. He watches Gabe break with sick satisfaction. When I look back at Gabe, his fingers are trembling as he wipes the sweat from his brow.

I can't even imagine how he's feeling. I ache for him. I want him to curl up with his head in my lap so I can soothe his bleeding heart.

"She died," Gabe says once he gains control of his emotions.

Jones nods. "She drowned less than a mile from where *you* directed the search."

Gabe mirrors his nod, both hands now supporting him on the console. "I remember now."

Jones crosses an ankle and cocks his head to the side. Unlike Gabe, his hands are steady as he caresses the gun on the table with a single finger. "Do you like playing God, Mr. Rossi? Do you like feeling in control of whether people live or die?"

"I—" Gabe struggles to find words and he scrubs a hand over his face. "I've never looked at it like that."

"No? You've never felt a rush when you're responsible for saving a life? Or ending one?"

"All I've ever wanted to do is help people," Gabe says, finally slinking to the floor as if his legs can no longer support his weight.

"You only had to keep searching," Jones says, his voice growing more urgent. "She was right there."

"I'm sorry," Gabe whispers.

"Sorry won't bring back my wife."

Sensing the situation is deteriorating, I turn to Jones. "What was her name?" I ask, grasping at the first question that comes to mind.

"Her name was Sheila," Jones says. The gun clatters against the table and he presses both fists into his eyes.

"How long were you married?"

Just keep him talking. If you can distract him, maybe someone will come.

At least, that's what I hope.

"We were married for nineteen years when she died."

"I'm so sorry," Gabe whispers.

Jones is across the room with his hands around Gabe's throat before I know what's happening. In seconds, Gabe's face goes from ghost-white to purple. Panicked, I look around the room for some way to help and I see that Jones has forgotten the gun on the table in his haste.

I stare at it for a few long heartbeats and then it's in my hand, heavier and bigger than I would have imagined. I flick off the safety and then cross the room.

Jones is still so intent on Gabe that he doesn't notice me until I press the muzzle against his head. "Let him go," I say, not recognizing the confident voice of the woman speaking.

Gabe's bloodshot eyes find mine and he shakes his head as much as he can with Jones' hands still around his throat.

Ignoring him, I jam the gun against Jones' skull. "I said, let him go."

"What are you gonna do with that, little girl?" Jones asks,

but his hands ease fractionally and Gabe's eyes find me over Jones' shoulder.

"I'm going to blow your head off if you don't let him go in the next ten seconds." Surprisingly, my hands are steady for the first time in hours as I nudge his shoulder with the gun. "Now, I said get up."

Jones waits a few seconds and then eases back on his haunches. "I should have killed you when I had the chance," he growls.

"Too late," I respond with a sickly sweet smile. Gabe coughs as he gets back to his feet. I offer him a hand up and say, "Are you okay?"

He does a weird shrug/nod that I take to mean yes. His feet are steady, but his eyes are still haunted. He gestures for the gun, but I hesitate for a second.

"I'm fine." He gestures again, and I hand it over. The gun in his hand restores some of his confidence and he straightens. "Get Tyler up on the line and tell him we're about fifteen miles northeast," he says.

"What are you gonna do?" Jones goads. "I don't think you actually have the balls."

Gabe points the gun at Jones' leg and fires off a round. I can't help my shriek of surprise—or the flinch. Jones howls and collapses on the floor.

"If you don't want me to give you an identical one in your other leg, remove this collar."

I gasp. "Gabe, no."

"It's fine," he says without looking at me.

"But he could detonate it."

He shakes his head as he and Jones share a long look. "He won't do that, will you Jonesy?"

"How could you possibly know he won't kill us all?"

Gabe's response chills me to my core. "Because he wants to see me suffer and an explosion would be over too quickly. Jones here says he's been planning this for a while. He wouldn't want it to end without having a little fun first."

"I don't—"

But Gabe doesn't listen. Instead, he crouches to where Jones is now kneeling on the floor and says, "Get the goddamn collar off of my neck or I will shoot you."

"Let me—"

"No," Gabe interrupts. "Me first. He needs me. He'd be too tempted to hurt you to spite me. He'll do me and then you'll explain to me how he did it, so I can take yours off next." When I don't move he stands, gun still trained on Jones, and his dark eyes come to me. "You understand?" he asks.

The words are stuck behind a tangle of fear in my chest. I know my eyes are wild and wide, but I nod anyway. Instinctively, I trust him like I've never trusted anyone before, in spite of the news about Jones' wife.

Gabe softens a little and hooks a hand around my neck. He forces me to look at him and then presses a soft, swift kiss to my lips, sending a shock throughout my entire body. My hands lift to guard against the onslaught, but end up gripping the still-slick material of his suit instead. Short though the kiss may be, it is unequivocally shattering.

When he releases me the barest of seconds later he positions me behind his back. I'm both numb and electrified and the combination short circuits my thoughts until I hear Jones working on the collar around Gabe's neck. My breath catches in my throat as Jones carefully maneuvers around the inner workings of the collar. Gabe and I hold a collective breath when the catch releases. I can't even bear to look.

A few seconds later, I peer through one eye and find Gabe rubbing his naked neck with one hand. The collar dangles from two long, tan fingers and he holds the gun loosely in his other hand.

Jones looks up at him, his face carefully blank. "What now, Gabe?"

Gabe sets the collar down carefully on the table, then gestures with the gun. "You're not done yet, Mr. Jones. Her next. I hope you have steady hands."

"Great," I mutter as I move next to him.

"Did you talk to Ty?" Gabe asks as he moves behind me.

"No," I hiss back, "I was too worried about the bomb around your neck."

He puts a hand on my back and nudges me forward. "I'm right here, Chloe."

I'm pretty sure I don't breathe until Gabe leans forward and says, "That's it. You're okay."

There's the slightest moment where a weight is lifted off my neck—both figuratively and literally—and then I get thrown backward, knocking Gabe down along with me.

Maybe the son-of-a-bitch detonated the bomb anyway.

CHAPTER NINE

GABRIEL

COLD.

Everything is cold.

Cold and numb.

I'd give anything for just a few minutes under the hot desert sun. I'd take the bombs, the endless, desolate panoramas, and even one hell of a dust storm for one ray of sunlight.

Something.

Anything to warm up my icy insides again.

The phone is ringing.

Is Emily calling?

Shit, was I supposed to pick her up today? Taylor will be pissed.

I sit up and my head spins.

God, I must have drank too much.

A hand shakes me and my traumatized brain conjures up a picture of a beautiful woman, all doe eyes and long hair.

Chloe.

I shoot straight up, ignoring the vicious pounding in my head. The ringing wasn't coming from a phone. It's coming from my own ears. Chloe is laying across my legs, her eyes fluttering, and soft groans bubbling up from her throat. Then her eyes open and she looks right at me.

"What the hell happened?" she asks, her voice cracking. She wets her lips with the tip of a pink tongue and lifts her uninjured hand to her brow.

Remembering Jones pushing Chloe, who knocked me down, I scan the wheelhouse and find it empty.

"Shit!" I get to my feet and offer her my hand. She looks up at me as she takes it and I pull her up. "The bastard just can't help shoving you, can he? I'm going to kick his ass."

"Where'd he go?" she asks.

"If he's smart, he jumped ship." I go to the fridge where I found his store earlier and find the gun still there. *Finally*, something goes right today. "Do you see where the other gun went?"

She glances around, confused. "I must have dropped it when he pushed me over."

A quick glance around the room and the gun doesn't turn up. "Best to assume he has it."

"Gabe," Chloe says.

I cross to the dashboard and radio Tyler. The line crackles but is otherwise silent.

"Gabe!"

I radio Tyler again, but still no response. Chloe yanks at my shirt and I turn around ready to snarl. "What the fuck?"

"The captain," she hisses and forces my head around with her hands.

The space where he was propped up against the wall is vacant and he's nowhere else in sight. I stride back across the room and rip the radio off its hook. "Tyler, it's Gabe, are you there?"

"Gabe, we're here," the radio crackles.

"Thank God." I give him our location and as I'm in the middle of relaying what's happened since we last spoke, I hear the ping of a bullet off of the dashboard. I drop the mic and cover Chloe's body with my own, but not before the next whizzing bullet causes her to cry out in pain.

I don't even notice when a third cuts a path of fire through my side or when a fourth shatters the glass above the dash, causing it to rain down on us.

"Are you—"

"If you ask me if I'm okay again, I'll strangle you myself," she says. "It's just a scratch."

I push my own injuries to the back of my head. "If you say so." Pressing Jones' gun into her hands, I shelter her with my body and urge her toward a wall for more cover. "I sure hope you know how to use this."

"Point and shoot, right?" she asks.

Even if I had the time, it's not worth it to argue. "Basically," I say. "Aim for his middle. Otherwise you're bound to miss."

"Do you think he will hurt the captain?" Chloe asks.

"I think he'll do whatever he can. He's desperate. I also think you should stay here while I go try to find where he's hiding."

Her fingers dig into my arm. "I don't think that's such a good idea. He's got a gun."

My teeth flash and I gesture to the firearm I found in the refrigerator. "So do I."

"We should wait until Tyler gets here with the sheriff's."

"If we do that, then Jones will kill him."

"And if you do this, Jones will kill *you*."

I tuck a strand of her hair behind her ear. "We don't have another choice."

She squares her shoulders. "Fine, but I'm going with you."

"I don't think so."

Her eyes flash and her pouty lips pull into a frown. "It's not up to you," she says and then skirts around me.

I grab her arm and she struggles against me. "The hell it isn't. You're not fucking going anywhere."

She gets in my face. "I think I've proved today that I won't run away from this guy. I can either go with you now, or follow you once you leave, but either way, you aren't leaving me behind," she says, then gives a pointed look at my hand still around her arm. "You can let go of me now."

When I don't, she frowns up at me.

"I'm thinking about it," I say.

She tugs her arm, but gets nowhere. "Better think fast."

"You're making me wish I was a cop so I could handcuff your ass where you'd be safe."

She tugs her arm again and this time, I let her go. As she rubs her wrist, she glares up at me. "My dad was a cop. I've got my own damn handcuffs."

I open my mouth to respond and then my jaw clamps closed. Blindly, I turn around and stride to the stairs as I gulp for air. *Jesus Christ.*

Surviving a psychopath hell-bent on my destruction is easy, but surviving Chloe is something else altogether.

"Gabe?" she whispers from behind me.

"Don't talk," I say through gritted teeth.

"It wasn't your fault," she says anyway.

The stairs are empty and they end in a square of flooring with yellow light pooling in the center. Smears of blood streak across from the woman Jones shot. The only thing in our line of sight is the woman's red heel poised drunkenly on its side.

"Stay behind me and for God's sake don't shoot me on accident," I tell her.

I ignore her muttered, "I might just shoot you on purpose," and focus on each step down. When I reach the bottom, I scan the shadowed main floor and find it empty.

"As if this whole night weren't creepy enough," Chloe says.

"Be quiet," I hiss.

But she's right. Ancient sconces adorn every other pole

and the light is so weak it only illuminates the area directly underneath it, leaving large spaces consumed by shadows.

Jones could be in any of them. Watching, waiting. Like a malignant tumor just biding time until it steals up on you when you least expect it.

Part of my job, though, has always been to expect the unexpected. Adapt. Overcome. I don't know how I'll live with the bombshell Jones dropped, but I'll worry about the implications later. The most important thing is getting Chloe off this boat alive. She's innocent in this.

My head aches, my side is on fire, and there's still a slight ringing in my ears, but I set all of that aside. To my right, there's another door that leads down into the engine access area, but I doubt he'd go down there. He'd be cornered, no way to escape. All the same, I put my back to the water so I can limit the points of attack.

The crash of water against the side of the ferry doesn't help. I'm down nearly two senses with the lack of light and the ringing so I move toward the back of the boat on pure instinct. Chloe moves behind me, silent as a breeze.

And then I hear it. It's barely higher than a whisper, but the sound of low voices is unmistakable.

"You go now," a man says. It's too low for me to discern if it's Jones or the captain.

"No," comes another voice.

I stop in my tracks and hold up a hand, signaling Chloe to wait. She nods in return and grips her gun a little tighter. The voices are coming from the back of the boat and grow louder as we near.

"Now," the first voice says.

"I'm not—"

A garbled yell cuts off his words and then even his hoarse cries are swallowed by the resulting crash of his body against the water. Chloe and I share a look.

"Jones must have pushed the captain overboard," she says. "Why would he do that?"

"Desperation," I guess. "He may be running out of ammo. We have his other weapons. Maybe he's trying to lure us out of hiding. It could be any one of a million things."

Silence presses in around us as I strain to hear any sign of movement. Then, the crack of a gun sounds through the night.

CHLOE

At first, I think the gunshot went wild and a rush of relief streaks through me. I slump against Gabe's back, my forehead lolling between his broad shoulders. His warmth and his closeness are immeasurably reassuring.

It takes a few seconds for me to register the liquid on my hands isn't spray from the ocean. Absently, I bring my hands up under a near spray of light and find them covered in red.

My eyes widen and I duck around Gabe to find his face awash with anguish. I thought I could handle traumatic. Apparently, I've got a hidden talent for it. Guns, bombs, murder. But my kickass girl-power persona melts away when he goes limp against me.

I catch him, his weight listing heavily against the metal railing beside us. "Gabe?" I whisper.

His heart thunders beneath my hands and his chest heaves in an effort to catch his breath. He opens his mouth like he wants to talk, but a hiss of pain escapes instead and his knees buckle.

My own breath hitches in my throat and tears prickle the back of my eyes. "Gabe?"

His weight takes us both down to the cold, wet floor and I do my best to control our descent but he's six-foot-two of pure male muscle and I'm one hundred twenty pounds soaking wet. His head bumps against the rail and he makes a pained sound in the back of his throat.

He can barely keep his head up and his lips are pulled too tight to talk. It's pitch black and I can't even see a foot in front of my face, so I can't see where he's injured.

"Gabe?" I say, and this time I can't even hear my own voice over the sound of the waves. "I'm going to check to see where you're hurt."

He makes a sound, but I can't tell if it's a warning or an assent. We don't have time for me to second guess myself, and if he's wounded he certainly doesn't have time for it, so I take a deep breath, but it does nothing to calm my nerves. Then all I can do is start.

His hair is shorn closely to his head and aside from a goose egg, there aren't any other serious injuries. I probe the bump, which makes him wince and rear back.

"Sorry," I say, pulling my shaking hands back. "I'm sorry."

"It's fine," he manages, his breath shallow. "Leg. It's—leg."

"Leg," I repeat. "Okay, right."

As I move down, my hand bumps against his midriff and he sucks in a quick breath.

"What are you..." My stomach drops when my hands come back soaked in what must be blood.

"He shot you twice?" I say incredulously. "Jesus Christ, Gabe. You aren't superman. Why didn't you say anything?"

"Put...pressure on it."

"Oh, I'll put pressure on it," I mutter. "I'm gonna help you with your zipper so I can wrap your wound up."

"Don't...have time. Need to...find Jones."

"Yeah, you sure as hell won't have time if you bleed out. Just shut up while I do this, then we'll go find Jones."

"Bossy," he says and I can hear the smile in his voice.

"Damn straight," I say. "Now shut up."

I unzip his wetsuit slowly, afraid of what I'm going to find underneath. My eyes adjust to the dark the hem of the suit reveals a track wound maybe four inches long through the fleshy part of his waist, I suck in a breath. I let it out in one shaky exhalation.

"Well, the good news is that it doesn't look deep," I say. "The bad news is that you've definitely been shot."

"Not the first time," he manages grimly.

"Now the part where you don't like hospitals is starting to make sense," I say.

I feel like a heroine in a Regency novel as I rip off the bottom part of my dress off to wrap around his waist. "I'm going to do this quickly," I say.

"Just do it."

I have to wedge my arms behind him to wrap the large strip around his stomach. The slash through his sides starts by his right hip and wraps around his side to end near his back. I fix the wide part of the strip over the wound and carefully align it to make sure it's completely covered before I arrange it on the other side and tie it off. I do it more tightly than I think is necessary because I have a feeling he's not going to take a few minutes to rest, even if we could.

I help him get his wetsuit back on as quickly and painlessly as possible. When I glance back up, I catch him grinning at me. "What?"

"You're not a nurse are you?" he jokes even though he's short of breath and grimacing in pain.

"Definitely not," I say.

He chuckles. "Maybe you should be. I wouldn't have such a bad attitude about them if I had a pretty nurse like you."

"You must be going into shock," I say and look away so he can't see the reluctant smile pulling at my lips. "Now be quiet. I've got to concentrate."

"Yes ma'am," he drawls.

My fingers tremble as I check over his leg. The material of his suit wicks away moisture, but it's slick on his outer thigh. I tear off another strip of my dress and wrap it around his leg.

"Not normally how I get women out of their clothes."

A laugh catches in my chest and I glance over at him as I tie off the tourniquet around his leg wound. "I think the knock on the head may have damaged your brain." Once the cloth is tied, I sit back on my heels. "Okay, it's not pretty and if you don't get medical treatment soon, I'm sure you'll risk infection or worse, but I think it'll do for now."

"You did great," he says.

"Thanks." I cross to his other side and wedge my shoulder under his arm to help him up. "Now let's find this guy and get the hell out of here. Where do you think he is?"

Gabe hisses in pain as he gets to his feet. "Well, he knows we're here, and he hasn't come to finish us off."

Without saying a word, we both head to the back of the boat where we heard Jones push the captain overboard. It's an arduous process. Gabe can only put so much weight on his wounded leg and I'm no match for his sheer bulk.

By the time we reach the back railing, we're both covered in sweat and panting, but the loading point is blessedly empty. One look at Gabe's face has me propping him against the railing. I look around and find a barrel for him to sit on and drag it over to him.

"Sit down before you pass out."

He glares at me, but collapses on the barrel anyway. "I'm fine," he insists.

"Yeah," I scoff. "You're so fine you're about to pass out

where you stand. Just, sit there. The Coast Guard should be here soon. As soon as they get here you can be all macho, but for now, just, don't."

I retrieve the gun from where I'd stored it in my cardigan's pocket and hold it loosely in my hand. The last thing I want to do is be caught off guard. Not knowing where Jones is at is making me jumpy and there's nothing in the water behind us except the waves. No sign of the captain.

"C'mere," Gabe says behind me.

I back up toward him, keeping my eyes on the boat in front of us. The shadows and moonlight are playing tricks on my eyes. Every whisper of wind or shifting light has all of my muscles tensing.

When I get close enough, Gabe tugs me back against him. He's shivering, probably from a combination of cold, fear, and pain. The tattered suit he's wearing isn't much of a barrier from the elements.

"They'll be here soon," I tell him. As I press my body into his uninjured side, I try not to think about how hard he is—all over, or how good he smells. So not the time.

"I should be the one rescuing you," he says and it makes me smile a little to hear the petulant tone in his voice.

"Trust me, I'm happy to be your damsel in distress if it'll get us off of this thing," I say.

"Definitely no damsel. You're more like a warrior queen," he says. His voice is soft. I don't know if it's because we're so close or because he's in pain. "Don't tell me you're a police officer, too."

The thought teases laughter out and I blush. "No, definitely not. I went to college for business management and I work at a luxury travel company out of Jacksonville."

"After this," he says, "I think we both deserve a vacation."

"Only if it doesn't involve boats."

A movement out of the corner of my eye catches my attention. My body goes rock solid, alerting Gabe, and he straightens. "See something?" he whispers, all playfulness gone from his voice.

I strain to make anything out of the darkness. "Not sure. I thought I did," I whisper back.

Shadows shift and Jones appears with his hands up, which makes the hand holding the gun pointed at his head sag.

"Oh my God," I say, once he gets close enough for me to see what had taken him so long.

Jones has his hands held over his head and in them is the control for the bomb collars he'd had the hostages wear. And around his neck is a collar of his own.

CHAPTER TEN

GABRIEL

AT FIRST I think I'm imagining things again, but Jones doesn't fade away like a bad dream. No. He's one hundred percent, hard to believe reality. He strides unerringly forward with another one of his goddamned bombs strapped to his neck.

"No wonder he took so long." Chloe shrinks back against me. "He was putting one of those things on. Why would he do that?"

He's only a few steps away now, close enough for us to see the gray pallor of his face in the spotty lighting. He looks about as good as I feel.

"What the hell are you doing, Jones?" He stops a couple yards away. I may want to throttle the life out of him, but I also have the innate urge to help him.

Jones' voice is calm when he speaks, despite how peaked

he looks. "When I lost my wife, I had nothing left. You took everything from me."

Chloe opens her mouth to talk, but I wrap an arm around her waist and tug her even closer against my body, cutting off whatever she was about to say.

I keep my response level and calm. There is still the possibility he'll set off his own collar while standing just a short distance away from us. "I'm sorry, Jones. I swear, we did everything we could to save your wife."

Jones just shakes his head sadly. "If what you're saying were true, she'd still be here."

"I wish I could change what happened." The intense regret is causing physical pain. My chest is tight and my throat aches.

"I didn't bring you out here for you to do anything."

My brows furrow. "Then why did you go to all this trouble?" If it wasn't to kill me, to hurt me, then why the hell are we here?

"I want you to understand."

"Then make me understand," I bite out.

"That's the idea," Jones says, and he inches closer.

"Stop right there," I say, but he keeps coming toward us. To Chloe, I say, "If he gets too close, shoot him."

His hands are still up, but with the explosives strapped to his neck, I'm not taking any chances. If he weren't holding the detonator, I would have instructed Chloe to shoot him, but I can't. I'm no bomb expert and I'm not going to start pretending to be now.

As Chloe trembles against me, I wonder for the first time if I'd caused more trouble coming out here to save her than I would have if I'd let the sheriffs and F.B.I. handle the situation.

"What do you want me to understand?" I ask. "I'm sorry, I can't tell you how sorry I am—"

"I don't want your sorries," Jones says sharply. "I wanted you to know what it felt like to have someone you cared about taken from you because of someone else's callousness."

I double over in pain as Emily's face comes to mind. Without thinking about it, I squeeze Chloe tighter against me and press an absentminded kiss into her hair. I say a silent thanks for her thoughtless actions that kept Emily from this nightmare. If nothing else, I'm immeasurably grateful for her bravery.

"And now?" Chloe's hand finds my arm. Her nails dig into the skin, but I barely feel it.

"Now, he'll get to know the same callousness," he says.

My mind blanks with panic, thinking somehow he got to Emily without my knowing. It's the two-second pause that catches me off-guard. Jones uses it to his advantage and he rushes toward us. Chloe yelps and lets off a couple rounds in quick succession. One wings him, but the other two are off the mark.

Jones stumbles, but regains his footing and then he's within reaching distance. I can see the whites of his eyes, he's so close. Then he's throwing the device toward us and we reel back, letting him leap off the back of the ferry and into the dark water below.

Chloe screeches and catches the device with her free hand, fumbling a little. We both spin around and search the white caps for his head.

"There!" Chloe says, pointing at a slightly less black blob about twenty feet away. The boat is still anchored to the ocean floor, but the current is rapidly pulling Jones' body farther and farther away. It takes a few seconds until my brain puts two and two together.

"NO!"

"What?" Chloe asks. "What is it?"

"The device," I whisper. "He'll set off his bomb himself. The water is going to carry him outside of range. He's trying to commit suicide. "

Her eyes widen and her mouth parts. "No."

Knowing what's coming, I tug Chloe into a squatting position behind the railing. It doesn't take long; it couldn't have been more than a handful of minutes from when we spotted Jones to the sound of another explosion.

Chloe burrows into my side, whimpering, and I try to focus on her soft, sweet body and not the horror happening on the other side of the railing. The horror I'm responsible for.

I rock her gently, comforting us both. "Shhh," I say into her hair. "Shh, it's over now. It'll be okay."

"H-h-he..." she sobs. "W-why would he...I don't understand."

I swallow around the lump in my throat, but when I talk,

my voice still breaks. "I-I don't know." I think she knows I'm lying, but she doesn't call me out on it.

There's an explicit emptiness in my chest and an iciness that has nothing to do with my wounds and blood loss. It doesn't take me long to piece together that the feeling is what Jones wanted me to understand.

Because it wasn't just his wife's blood on my hands. Now it's his, too.

An indeterminable amount of time later, Chloe helps me to my feet. She's talking to me in a soothing voice, but I'm not listening and I don't try to add to her one-sided conversation.

"Let's get you back up to the wheelhouse, then we can radio Tyler and see where the hell the backup is. They would have heard the explosion by now, they should be here."

The good thing about how I'm feeling is that I can't feel anything at all. Including my gunshot wounds. Before, I could barely stay conscious they were so painful. Now...nothing.

There's nothing.

Somehow she shoulders my weight until we get up the stairs and in the wheelhouse. Sensing my uselessness, Chloe deposits me on an empty chair and goes straight to the radio to call for Tyler.

My ears are ringing again, so I don't hear their conversation. The only thing I can hear is the sound of Jones' voice and the loud *boom* from the explosion that killed him.

Chloe's feet appear in my line of vision and I follow her legs up to her waist and finally to her concerned face.

"I'm fine," I croak out, but I don't think she believes that either.

"They're on their way. About ten minutes out. There were a lot of injuries from the last explosion and red tape to wade through. They haven't found the captain yet, but they'll send a search team out for him, too."

I nod, but I don't say anything. When the silence stretches between us, Chloe hops back up and says, "I'm going to see if I can figure out how to lift the anchor so we can meet them halfway."

I close my eyes. Try as I might, when I try to call up Sheila Langford-Jones' face, I can't.

And it's almost as bad as being responsible for her death.

I should remember her face. I have a vague recollection of a middle-aged woman, maybe dark hair? But aside from that, there's not much else wiggling free in my fuzzy memories.

What bothers me is what I can remember. The weather. I can barely recall the face of the woman who died, but I can remember the goddamned weather. The awesome force of the gale that swept her boat out to sea. I remember the search grid. I remember the people, all of them, who are assigned to my team.

Apparently I can remember all of the things that didn't matter, but the one supposed to be the most important of all, I don't.

"Shit!" Chloe's shriek breaks me out of my reverie.

I look up and find the wheelhouse empty. The hot lance

of fear stabs through me so intensely, I'm up and across the room before a clear thought crosses my brain.

"Chloe?" I shout down the stairs. I take a few steps down and shout again. "Chloe!"

Her shadowed form appears at the bottom of the stairs. Her face is so white I can see it even though there are no lighted pillars near her.

"What's wrong?" I ask.

She opens her mouth like she's going to say something, but a choked sound is all that comes out. I start to go down the stairs to meet her, but she seems to shake herself out of it and she races up the stairs and past me.

"Chloe," I say again. "What's wrong?"

She doesn't answer me. Instead she fumbles with the radio mic again and keys it up. "Tyler?" She slaps an impatient hand on the console and whispers "C'mon, c'mon" beneath her breath. "Tyler are you there?"

A garbled sound answers her and I take slow measured steps toward her. I didn't think our situation could possibly get worse, but I should have known Jones wouldn't let me off the hook so easily.

"We have a major problem," she tells him. There's another garbled response and then her shoulders heave as she steadies herself. "You guys need to keep back," she says.

This time I can hear Tyler's response because I've been taking steps closer without even thinking about it. "Keep back?" Tyler says. "What the hell are you talking about,

Chloe? We need to get you two off of there. Gabe needs medical attention."

"You can't come near us." She runs a shaking hand over her hair. "There's a huge bomb in the engine room."

CHLOE

"What the hell do you mean there's a bomb in the engine room?" Gabe demands, his pale face flushed red.

I flick a glance at him and then depress the button on the mic. "Tyler, you have to keep everyone away from here."

"Motherfucker!" Gabe exclaims behind me.

"What if we come up behind—"

"There's no time." I picture the small bundle of black I found in the engine room, it's red face flashing with menace. "There's a timer on the bomb. We only have seven minutes. I managed to get the anchor up so we can keep heading out to sea. I don't want anyone to get hurt."

"What about you two?" Tyler demands. "We have to get you off of there."

"Don't worry about—"

"No," Gabe interrupts. He leans heavily against the console and snatches the mic from my now ice-cold hands. To Tyler, he says, "Do you have any speedboats out there?"

"We've got whatever you need," Tyler says.

"Send the fastest one you've got, but be careful. Chloe's is going to jump ship and I don't want you to run her over." He meets my gaze and then says, "She's precious cargo."

"Do you—"

"We don't have time to debate," he tells Tyler. "Get them here now."

Gabe drops the mic and wipes his forehead. "We've got to get you out of here. Can you swim?"

"Can I swim?" I repeat.

Gabe cups my head with a hand and presses a quick, hard kiss on my stunned lips. "Baby, we don't have time. Need an answer now. Can you swim?"

"Yes," I say, dazedly. "I can swim." A wave of exhaustion crashes over me and I sway.

His head jerks up. "What?"

Tears burn, but I will them away. "I don't know how long I'm gonna be able to. Getting kind of worn out here."

Darkness flashes in his eyes, then a second later it's gone. He searches about the cabin and finds an orange life vest. With great care, he slips it around my shoulders and buckles it at the waist. "You promise me," he says, his attention completely focused on securing the buckles and tightening the straps. "Promise me once you're in the water you'll swim, fast as you can, away from this damn boat."

"What will you do?" His wounds aren't going to do well in the water and I see the reflection of my thoughts in his eyes.

He tucks the strap in and he threads his hands through my hair. When he speaks, his voice is gruff, detached, but I can intuit the lack of emotion is because if he were to betray any at all, neither of us would make it out of this alive.

"I'm gonna make sure no one else gets hurt. I've got to

make sure this thing isn't going to drive straight into someone so I'm gonna point it far out to sea to make sure no one gets in its path."

"What about you? You're coming with me, right? We don't have much time now."

"You don't need to worry about me," he responds as he turns away to secure the steering wheel. "Go," he says gruffly. "Go now."

"I can't leave you," I say and it's true. My feet are glued to the ground. I couldn't leave even if I tried.

He slams his palms against the wheel. "Don't be stupid. Get the fuck off of this boat before the damn thing explodes."

But I'm shaking my head. "You'll have to throw me off the damn thing because I'm staying."

A pained expression flits over his face, breaking his calm facade. He strides over and takes me by the arm, but I surprise us both with a last summoning of strength. He grips my biceps with enough force to leave bruises and shakes me like a rag doll.

"Stop being so fucking stubborn!"

I ball my fists up and glare at him defiantly. "You didn't leave me," I spit back at him. "You're the one who's being stupid if you think I won't let you commit suicide. Either you come with me or neither of us are getting off of this boat."

"If you don't go now, you won't make it," he growls.

I meet his gaze. "Then, I guess you'd better get started, huh?"

He holds my eyes for a few seconds longer, then he bites

off a curse and spins around. While he's working at the dash directing the ferry way out to sea, I take a quick search around the cabin. It's in shambles, but there has to be something here we can use.

First, Gabe needs his own life vest. With his wounds, he'll last even less time than I will. I find one in a drawer and set it on the table. Next, I need something to signal the rescue boats with. My heart is beating so fast I think I may faint, but I force myself to focus. After a few frantic seconds of searching, I find a flashlight on top of a set of filing cabinets.

When I turn back, I find Gabe locking the wheel with the forked back of a chair. He sees me standing behind him and he sighs.

"I was kind of hoping you'd come to your senses," he says as he crosses the room, his limp growing more pronounced.

I hand him the vest but keep the flashlight. "Not a chance." I glance at the clock on the dash and say. "We better get moving. We've got about five minutes left and I'd rather not be here for too much longer."

Gabe finishes buckling his life vest and then he cups my cheek. It may be the shock of all the traumatic events of the day. I could reason it away as some sort of reverse Stockholm syndrome where I start to have feelings for my rescuer. But whatever the reason, when he tips my gaze up to his, time stops.

"I'm gonna crank up the speed, it won't be much, but we need to put as much distance between us and this rig as possible. Once I do, we need to hightail it out of here, 'kay?" I nod and he heaves a breath. "Good," he murmurs. "Good."

He turns and puts the throttle wide out. When he turns back, I take my place under his arm and help him to the stairs. Our progress down them is a slow, arduous process and I can feel each and every second pass with slow, aching precision.

Gabe's face is tight with grim determination and by the time we reach the bottom, it's also ghost white. Fear, not for the bomb, not for me, but for him, burns through me, revitalizing my resolve.

I ignore the screaming pain in my legs and the blackness encroaching on my vision. Through sheer strength of will, I shoulder Gabe down the long length of the first floor until we're at the back railing where Jones threw himself overboard.

Pushing those thoughts from my mind, I carefully lean Gabe against the railing and undo the latch for the gate used to load and unload passengers. It squeals at it swings wildly out.

I turn to Gabe and give him a weak smile. "Are you ready?" I ask.

"Hell, no," he says, but he holds his hand out anyway.

"You need to go first," I say as I take it.

A shock of panic courses through me when he doesn't even argue with me. He's too tired to even talk back and that's when I worry he may be worse off than I thought.

Gabe inches to the open gate and his shoulders lift as he inhales deeply. He gives me one long, searching look before he throws himself off of the edge.

I rush to the railing just in time to see him disappear beneath the water. Without giving myself time to think about it, I hurl myself down after him. A scream tears itself from my throat as I go down, down into the freezing cold depths of the water.

The impact knocks the breath out of me and the water tosses me in every direction. I open my eyes to the sting of the water, but it's useless. I can't see anything. The vest tugs me upward and I swim one-handed, the other weighed down by the bulky flashlight. I can only hope it's waterproof as I surge to the top.

I gulp in air and seawater as waves knock me back and forth. Twisting around, I scan the surface for a sign of Gabe, but it's hard to see anything. With my free hand, I pull myself in a random direction. Behind me, the boat speeds off into the darkness, a flame on top of the water.

"Gabe!" I choke on water and spit it out. "Gabe!"

Remembering the flashlight, I flick the switch and am filled with relief when it illuminates a swath in front of me.

"Gabe!"

I scan the light over the surface, but the darkness makes it pretty impossible to see much. He could be anywhere. Spinning around in every direction, waving the light frantically, I'm overcome with the fear. If he succumbed to his injuries and gone under while I was searching, I'll never find him. Over the waves, I can hear the sound of a clock ticking down precious seconds.

My arms turn to cement from pulling myself through the

waves and holding up the hefty flashlight, but I keep going. Finally, my light snags on a blob that doesn't match the water around it.

"Gabe!" By now my voice is hoarse, but I keep screaming his name hoping it'll rouse him. "Gabe!"

When I finally get to him, I nearly go under when I realize he's floating face down in the water and he's completely limp.

CHAPTER ELEVEN

GABRIEL

EVERYTHING IS MUFFLED and I'm so cold, it's almost hot, like when I played in snow for the first time as a kid and forgot to wear gloves. I know I need to get up, but I'm so tired, I sink back into darkness. I hear someone calling for me, but I can't summon the energy to figure out who it is and why.

"Gabe!" They call again.

Then hands are on me, turning me over and I realize I can't breathe. Coughing overcomes me, my body trying to purge my lungs of its contents.

"Gabe, oh my God," a woman says.

I blink, trying to pull her face into focus, but it takes so much energy I give up and pull a picture of her to the forefront of my memory. *Chloe.* Tyler always says if he's going to die, he'd rather do it staring at a beautiful woman. I'll have to remember to tell him he's right. After a few seconds of furious hacking and blinking, my lungs clear and my vision refocuses.

"You're okay," Chloe says. "We're okay."

"S'goin' on?" I slur.

"It's okay. We're safe. The boat—" But an explosion cuts off her words. Waves of heat pass over us and debris rains down around us.

She loses her grip on me and the water swallows me, despite my life jacket. At least this time I manage to hold my breath until she finds me and drags me back to the surface. We break through the top and float there for a second watching the decimated wreckage of the ferry be consumed by tongues of flames.

When we can tear our eyes away, Chloe turns to me and says, "Are you okay? They should be here soon."

It takes me a couple tries with my teeth chattering from the cold, but I spit out, "F-fine. I'm fine."

"You don't look fine," she says.

A bead of water drips down her face, and I wish I had the energy to trace its path with my fingers.

I shake my head to clear it. "I'll be okay."

A feeling I don't quite recognize is filling my chest, making it tight and hard to breathe. For a second, I wonder if Jones had gotten off another shot that we missed. My face grows hot and my throat scratchy. I keep trying to cough to clear it out, but it comes back.

"Just hold on," Chloe is saying, her face illuminated by the distant fire. "I can hear them. They're getting closer."

I have to focus intently on the sound of the water and my own racing heart, but I do catch the faintest sound of an engine roaring and it does sound close. Relief steals over me.

"They're almost here," Chloe says.

I try to find them in the darkness, but my vision is failing. Maybe Jones did get another shot off. Or maybe my bandages came off and I'm bleeding out.

"Stay with me," is the last thing I hear Chloe say before I pass out.

———

"You're damn lucky," Tyler says.

I glance around the hospital room, at the wires and tubes connecting me to a half-dozen machines and then back at him. "Lucky?" I say.

"Coulda been worse," he says.

Leaning into the soft, but thin, pillows, I grunt. "Yeah, it could have. Almost was."

A knock comes at the door and a cheerful-looking nurse peers around the edge with Tyler's wife following close behind holding two cups of coffee. "Mr. Rossi, just need to come check you over."

The nurse is young, mid-twenties maybe and the type of woman I would have hit on and tempted back to my place. As she inspects my bandages, even flipping up the sheets to look at the gunshot wound on my leg, I don't feel the slightest stirring of lust. Nothing.

Probably because they haven't told me anything about Chloe. I'm exhausted, I tell myself. I'll be able to relax when I know she's okay and then I can go home and life will go back to normal. Whatever normal is.

"Looks good, but take it easy," the nurse says and then shoots a stern look at Tyler. "You need to rest, Mr. Rossi."

Tyler holds his hands up in defense and gives her an easy smile. "I'll make sure he doesn't move," he tells her.

His wife rolls her eyes and smacks the back of his head after the nurse closes the door behind her. Tyler smiles wider and kisses his wife on her lips, murmuring to her.

"When are they letting you out?" his wife asks when she can pull herself from Tyler's grip.

I shrug before I forget about the gash in my side. "Probably tomorrow. They've stitched me up, gave me antibiotics. Don't see any reason why I need to stay longer than that."

Selena raises her eyebrows. "Tomorrow, huh?" she says.

My lips twist into a scowl. "I'm not staying in here longer than that."

"He hates hospitals," Tyler tells her.

Selena says, "You were shot twice and nearly blown up, for God's sake. You need to rest like the nurse said."

I shake my head. "I won't get any rest here. It'd be best for all involved if I do my convalescing at home."

"You'll stay here until they discharge you," Selena says firmly.

Tyler gazes at her with moony eyes. "Gotta love her," he

says and kisses her hand. "She's a pain in the ass, but you gotta love her."

I roll my eyes at the both of them. "I'll stay," I say, then add, "for now."

Selena gives me a stern look, then kisses Tyler on the cheek. "I've got to get going, but you keep an eye on this guy and make sure he doesn't give those pretty nurses too much trouble."

Grateful for the change in subject, I say, "Yes, ma'am."

She comes to give me a kiss. "You rest, okay? I'm not joking."

"Fine," I say. "But only if you promise to run away with me. You deserve much better than that old man."

Tyler makes a scoffing sound in his throat.

Selena smiles again and ruffles my hair. "Get better," she says, "and we'll see."

Once she leaves, I'm able to unhinge my smile and I stare out of the window for a while. Tyler watches me silently until I say, "You don't have to stay. I'll be pretty boring for a while."

Tyler doesn't crack a joke, which isn't like him. "I think you need to talk about what happened," he says with an uncharacteristically serious face.

"I'm fine," I say to the wall over his shoulder.

"Cut the bullshit," he says. "You're not okay. I can look at you and see you're not okay."

"I don't want to talk about it right now."

"You can't cage that shit up," Tyler says. "You need to get

it out or it'll haunt you." When I say nothing, he keeps going. "It was about his wife, wasn't it? While I was waiting for them to bring you in, I looked him up. The Lady who drowned a while back? That was his wife?" He pauses like he's waiting for me to acknowledge him, but I keep my face carefully blank. "It doesn't take a genius to guess he blamed you for her death."

"Ty, I don't want to do this," I say.

"Then I'll talk." He crosses the room to sit beside me. "It wasn't your fault," he says.

"I know it's not my fault."

"Do you? Maybe you should tell that to your face, because you look like you killed twenty people instead of saving their lives."

"I didn't save them. I'm the reason he kidnapped them. If it wasn't for me, they would have been fine."

"The reason he kidnapped them is because he was a sick man," Tyler argues. "A sick man made that decision out of anger and grief. He wasn't right in the head, Gabe. If I lost Selena, I'd be mad as all hell, but I wouldn't kill people because of it."

I keep my eyes on the bedspread. I can't bring myself to look at him. "If she was caught in that storm and I couldn't get to her in time—"

"I wouldn't blame you," he says. "In our line of work, people die. That doesn't mean it was your fault. You tried to save her. You can't save everyone." There's silence while I digest his words. They make absolute sense, but that doesn't mean I believe them. "Just think about it," he says. "Besides, you saved everyone on that boat."

"Not everyone," I say.

"The city is planning on giving you a medal," Tyler adds and startles a disbelieving snort from me.

"You're kidding."

"Or maybe it's keys to the city."

I shake my head. "Unbelievable."

"No shit," he says. "Stevens about shit a brick."

"I bet." I try to keep the words inside, but my concern overrules my common sense. "How is she?" I ask.

"Why don't you go see her yourself?" he asks.

"Probably not a good idea."

Another knock comes at the door and I can see the top of Emily's head through the window. Taylor hovers close behind her.

Tyler twists to see them, then gives me a brotherly pat on the shoulder. "Just think about what I said," he tells me as he walks to the door. "Think about going to see the girl, too. I'm gonna go grab some coffee from the cafeteria. I'll be back."

He greets Taylor and Emily's squeal as she bursts through the door.

"Daddy!" she shouts as she throws herself bodily onto the bed next to me.

"Emily," Taylor chides. "Be careful, your daddy's hurt."

"Sorry, Daddy," Emily says, her sweet face upturned.

I brush her hair back from her flushed face. "That's okay, angel. I'm fine. I'm happy to see you."

"I'm glad you're okay," Emily says solemnly.

"Thank God you got back okay," Taylor adds. "After you left we were so scared. I shouldn't have convinced you to go."

I wave her concerns away. "I would have had to go anyway."

Taylor's face turns serious. "I heard."

Emily snuggles up next to my side and wraps her arms around me. I barely notice the twinge from my ribs. Her fruity shampoo calms me and I press my face closer to her head to inhale it.

"We can talk about it later," she says as she looks around the room. She takes in the dozens of vases of flowers on every available surface. "I see you've got admirers. It was a madhouse downstairs. There were ten or twelve reporters trying to get in."

"You guys okay to get home?" I ask.

She nods. "We'll be fine. We wanted to come and visit for a while."

"What about the girl, Daddy? Did you save her?"

I relax for the first time since I heard her voicemail. "I did, sweetheart. But I think she saved me, too."

CHLOE

I should be happy.

Really, I am.

"You're good to go, Ms. McKinney," a nurse says. She pauses in the doorway. "We're so happy that you're okay."

"Thank you," I tell her, but my voice sounds wooden to my ears. "Me, too."

The door closes behind her and I turn back to my study of the square of grass outside my window. It's lightening up outside, and I want to watch the sun come up. Maybe knowing that life will go on, that *my* life isn't over, will help eradicate the dull, cotton that's filled my chest.

It's over. It's over and you're fine.

No matter how many times I repeat those words, my brain doesn't quite seem willing to accept them. I tried going to sleep, but every time I laid my head down and closed my eyes, I could see Jones' face in my mind and I'd shoot up, expecting to find him grinning down at me. Eventually, I gave up trying to sleep and convinced a nurse to let me have a cup of coffee instead.

It's long since cooled on the bedside table because I found I couldn't stomach much of anything.

"Hey," comes a soft voice from the doorway.

I tear my gaze away from the window and find Sienna standing in the doorway. Her face is red, mottled, but dammit she looks beautiful even with splotchy skin and eyes bloodshot from crying.

She sniffles and wipes her nose with a tissue. "I'm so sorry," she says brokenly.

I sit on the foot of my bed and gesture for her to come inside. "I didn't know you were coming back! And you have nothing to be sorry about," I tell her. "This wasn't your fault."

"How can you say that?" she sobs. "I'm the one that told

you to take the job. I practically forced you! If it weren't for me, you would have been on vacation. Probably met some sexy beach bum. Instead, you nearly got k-killed."

"There's no way you could have known it was going to happen." I pull her down until she's sitting beside me. "Don't you dare blame yourself."

"How can I not?" she asks.

"Hey," I say, wrapping an arm around her shoulder. "I was the one nearly killed. What I say, goes." I intended it to be a joke to lighten the mood, but it causes her to burst into fresh tears.

"I'm s-sorry." She takes a shuddering breath. "I told myself I wouldn't cry, but when I saw your name on the news, I thought you were gonna die. I made them turn us around."

I wince. "I totally forgot. Did you find a place to stay?"

She shakes her head. "No, but that's not important. What's important is that you're okay. You're here."

"I'm okay." I rub her back.

Sienna laughs and gets to her feet. "Look at me. I'm in worse shape than you are. You don't look the least bit trauma-tized." Her eyes narrow. "Why don't you look traumatized?"

I lift a shoulder.

Sienna stops dabbing at her eyes and she squints at me. "There's something you're not telling me," she declares impe-riously. "What is it? What happened? You're not hurt are you? You look fine." She studies me for a few more seconds, then her mouth drops open into a little O of surprise. "No, you can't—did you meet someone? You look positively miserable."

Turning my back on her I cross back to the window to find the sun is rising over the buildings. "No, of course not."

There are few seconds of silence and then she makes a sound in the back of her throat. "No, I don't believe you. This is exactly how you looked when that asshole broke up with you. I don't—how the hell did you meet someone when you were a hostage? This isn't some sort of Stockholm situation, is it?"

That startles a laugh out of me. "No, it's not."

"Then who..." Her head jerks backward and she sucks in a breath. "That man," she says, "the one who saved you."

"Well, I like to think I helped."

"You've got the hots for your rescuer?" The thought seems even more ridiculous when she says it out loud. "The one they've been showing on the news?" She pauses thoughtfully. "He is pretty hot."

I glance over at her wondering if she's seen him. The question must show plainly on my face because she says, "They showed his picture during the news report. Yours, too, actually. You're all they've been able to talk about since it started."

"Did they—" My throat closes around the words so I clear it and force myself to continue. "Did they say if he was okay?" I hope the words don't sound as desperate and hopeful as I think they do.

"Oh, honey," Sienna says, coming up beside me to wrap an arm around my waist and watch the sunrise with me. "He's fine. The news report said he was wounded—they didn't specify how—but they said he'll be okay. I think he's here, too, because of the mob outside and the heavy police guard."

"Good—that's good. I'm glad."

"I don't mean to overstep my bounds because I'm sure you're overwhelmed as it is, but is he why you look so upset? Did he...do something?"

"No, no, of course not." I put a reassuring hand on her arm. "He was, is, great. I promise."

"Then what's the problem?" she asks.

"I just—this will sound stupid," I warn.

She laughs. "No judgment. If anyone will understand, it's me."

A knot loosens inside of me. I should have known I could confide in her. "Okay, well. I guess I want to see him again. Make sure he's okay for myself. When I saw him last they were loading his unconscious body into an ambulance after they rescued us and that's the image I have in my head of him, laying on the gurney looking like he died. He came to help me. I want to see him to make sure he's okay for my peace of mind."

She runs her fingers through my hair and for the first time since they rescued us from the water, I feel a sense of calm. "That makes total sense. He saved your life. I'm sure he wouldn't mind if you went over to visit him."

"Yeah..."

"But," she prompts.

"But maybe there might be some feelings in there somewhere."

Sienna squeals, then calms herself down. "I'm sorry. I—well I know how upset you've been since Thomas broke things off."

"Yeah, but, *ugh*, this is stupid. Tell me it's stupid. I don't want to make a fool out of myself if it's just, like a situation crush or something."

"Does it feel like a crush?" she asks.

"Not sure I trust my judgment right now."

"Maybe you should go see him and see how you feel."

I shrug. "I don't know. Maybe. Won't that be weird? It would be horrible if he was all business-like. I'd feel stupid."

"You'd be even more stupid if you do like this guy and you don't go see him. Maybe he feels the same way."

"He's got enough on his plate without me bothering him."

"If you say so, but I still think you should go see him."

A nurse knocks on the door with a tray for breakfast and I'm thankful as Sienna changes the subject.

I endured the horrors of last night, but the thought of putting myself out there and then being rejected like I was with Thomas is almost too much to bear.

CHAPTER TWELVE

GABRIEL

THE ROOM IS QUIET, too quiet.

It leaves me too much time to think. And my thoughts aren't happy ones.

I couldn't concentrate enough to watch any T.V. and none of the shows seemed interesting anyway. I wanted to ask Taylor to let Emily stay, but they were both exhausted and Emily needed to be somewhere familiar. There's no use upsetting her more than she already is.

It's been twenty-four hours since our rescue and I've thought of her at least a million times during every one. The doctors restricted me to the hospital bed for 48 hours of observation due to my injuries and the officers guarding my door won't let anyone but vetted personnel and my family in.

In short, I'm slowly going crazy.

It'd be a different story if I had something to occupy my

time other than quiet contemplation. I'd kill for a devastating hurricane or a capsized boat. Then I remember that I'm still recovering from the gunshots and my misery starts all over again. The only sleep I've gotten is medically induced and even then my nightmares wake me every couple hours.

This time, I didn't let the nurses give me a sedative. If I'm not gonna sleep, I'd rather do it without the grogginess that accompanies the medicine.

A knock comes at the door and I open my mouth to snarl at them when I recognize the dark, wavy hair. Of course, the last time I saw her she was in a torn, soaked dress the same dark blue of her eyes. She looks as beautiful as I remembered, even in a shapeless hospital gown.

"Hey," she says.

I sit up in the bed and hope I don't sound like an eager fuckin' teenager. "Hey."

She walks hesitantly to my bedside with her lip clamped between her teeth. My heart hammers in my chest, the first sign of life I've had since the boat exploded, as she sits down next to me. The bed shifts with her weight and I have to knot the bed sheets on the other side to keep from pulling her close.

"How are you?" she asks, pausing the gnawing on her lip enough to say the words and then her teeth take hold again.

"I'm—" I stop to wet my own lips to keep from tasting hers. The few kisses we'd shared didn't necessarily mean anything to her. They hadn't to me at the time, or so I thought. Now, I'm not so sure. Do I want them to? She damn sure deserves better than me. "I'm good. Doctor says I should make a full recovery."

"That's good news," she says.

"How about you? Gonna make it?"

"Looks like it," she says, shifting slightly on the bed so that our legs brush. She takes no outward notice of it, but my body goes electric. "How's the hospital treating you? Still hate them?"

"I don't know," I say, my eyes on her lips. "It's not so bad right now."

Her cheeks turn pink and her eyes drop to the thin comforter. "There's the Gabe I know," she says.

"Been missin' him, huh?" I tease.

Then she looks back up at me, and the smile fades from my lips and it becomes difficult to breathe.

"What if I was?" she asks, her voice soft.

I swallow, then say, "Then why didn't you come here sooner?"

She laughs. "I guess I didn't want to seem like a crazy person. I didn't want you to tell me to get lost."

I scoot over on the bed to make room for her, noting the dark shadows under her eyes. "I'd never tell you to get lost," I say and then tug on her arm. "Lie down with me."

She resists for a second and then caves. "You been able to sleep?" she asks as she reclines next to me. She takes care not to bump my wounds and then finally lays her head on my shoulder.

The bed isn't huge and the bars are pressing into my back,

but having her next to me is the most comfortable I've been in a long time.

"No," I say when I remember she asked me a question. "Not well and I hate medicine. If another person comes at me with a syringe of sedatives, I might have to tackle them to the ground to defend myself."

She laughs. "So you've been terrorizing the nursing staff."

The tension in my shoulders starts to dissolve and I relax into the bed. "I'd never do that," I say with a grin.

Chloe turns on her side and rests her head on my shoulder. "Sure you wouldn't."

I fake-scoff. "I don't think you've known me long enough to make those kinds of judgments, thanks."

She blinks up at me. "You're right."

My smile fades. "I didn't mean—"

"No," she interrupts with a giggle. "I don't mean that. I mean I don't know you. I mean we survived this horrible thing and I feel closer to you than I've ever felt with anyone." She pauses, her eyes widening with surprise and she glances away nervously. "I mean, not that we're close or anything, um, I mean that—"

I cover her mouth with my hand and she stops speaking, her gaze coming back to mine. "You don't have to explain," I say, my voice low.

"I don't?"

Her hair feels like silk in my hands and I murmur, "Mmh-mm," as I drape it over her dainty shoulders. She's a delicately made woman for someone so fierce. Remembering her guarding me with a gun makes me smile.

"What?" she asks, smiling back at me.

"Just remembering you protecting me with a gun. For someone so little you're pretty damn formidable."

"I'm not little," she says. "You're just huge."

Having her so close is doing ridiculous things to my body. I'd turned off all the lights to go to sleep so the lack of light is intensifying all of my other senses. I can smell the plain soap she must have used in the shower, which only serves to make my imagination run wild.

I gulp down air and try to refocus on the conversation. "What do you want to know?" I ask to get my brain to focus on something, anything, other than how she feels against me.

"Everything," she says.

___

In the hazy light of morning, I wake to find myself wrapped around a beautiful woman, slightly confused as to how I got there. I have one arm cradled underneath her head and the other slung around her waist so she's pressed against me in all the right places. And I mean *all the right places.* Her breath fans across the sensitive skin along my neck.

It takes a while for me to remember what happened and how she got into bed with me and then the previous night comes to me. We'd lain in the bed together for hours, just talking. It's been a long time since I had a woman in bed for a reason other than getting naked with her.

As I shift to put a little room between us, despite every instinct telling me not to, she makes a sound of protest and moves closer. She throws one of her thighs over my hip and— hand to God—I don't intend to kiss her again—at least not until we'd at least gone on an official date, but I do.

Her lips are unbelievably, exquisitely soft. A growl rumbles in my chest and her hand rises to press against it, hesitantly at first as she rouses. I watch as her eyes flutter open and catch mine. As they widen in surprise and then dilate with desire, my muscles steel with triumph.

I use the arm around her waist to my advantage, leveraging her weight until she's pressed as close as she can be. We both groan in unison at the sensitive contact, the simple touch reigniting the spark between us I've been trying so hard to ignore. The pain from my wounds is nonexistent. In its place is pure pleasure.

Her mouth opens and I cup her face with my hands, guiding her movements in tandem with mine. I touch, and taste, and go a little crazy with her kiss. Her fingers clutch at my shoulders as she does everything that she can to practically bind herself to me.

Desire flares white-hot between us and when I'm about to flip her to her back and show her how much I need her, she devastates me by breaking the kiss and sliding her lips along my jaw to my ear. She exhales an unsteady breath and nibbles at the sensitive skin there. My mind blanks and narrows to the simple, but effective point of contact.

How or why doesn't matter. What matters is the breathless way she whispers my name when I knot her hair in my hand to plunder her mouth. What matters is the way her heart stutters in her chest when I trail my lips on a path down her neck to the pink-splotched skin revealed by the thin hospital blanket.

I bring my lips back to her ear as my hand ghosts along her neckline. "Do you want me to stop, baby?" The question burns me when I ask; the last thing I want to do is stop. But even worse than that would be making a move she isn't ready for. I've got all the time in the world, I can wait. It'll probably kill me, but I can try.

She answers by plunging her hands into my hair and pulling my mouth back to hers. I respond by covering her body with my own. I hesitate for a moment, wondering if I'm moving too fast, doing too much, but she simply cradles me between her thighs, pulling me closer to her warmth. There's a twinge from my stitches, but I push that to the back of my mind.

It's been a long time since I've been with a woman I cared about—probably too long if I'm being honest. After my horrific divorce, relationships weren't high on my list of priorities. Maybe I was waiting for someone like Chloe. Someone soft and a little sweet, too idealistic for this shitty world, but at the same time, determined in her own right.

Her hands trail along my chest, and no fucking joke, my

breath catches in my throat at the hesitant touch of her fingers against my skin. I feel like a goddamned teenager necking in the living room and realize I must immediately shift the balance of power before I completely lose control.

CHLOE

I awaken to the warm, comforting feeling of being surrounded by a pair of strong arms. The scent he wears—whatever it is— is like an aphrodisiac. I can't get close enough. Then his lips are on mine and I forget everything but how it feels to fall.

The world around us fades like a watercolor. The only sensations I'm aware of are the press of his lips against mine, the stubble on his jaw as it scrapes a line down my throat and the sound of the growl in his chest as our bodies press together.

I have to taste more of him so I break the kiss to nibble my way up to his ear and his body vibrates against me. I press my lips to the curve of his neck and inhale deeply. I'm certain then, as sure as I am of my own name, that I will never forget his scent. I'll be rolling down an aisle at the grocery store and catch the slightest whiff of his cologne and be immediately transported back to this moment.

His mouth travels down my body and then he pauses to ask if this is okay. My only answer is bringing his lips back to mine.

I don't know how long we lie there, getting to know one

another, learning each other's bodies and responses. We could stay here forever and I wouldn't give a damn.

It's been so long since I've felt wanted like this. No, *needed*. When was the last time a man held on to me like he couldn't let go? I wrap my arms around him and plunge my fingers into his hair, suddenly frantic at the thought of losing this feeling.

He pulls back to break the contact and sits up. I blink blearily up at him. His face appears haloed in a beam of early morning sunlight dappling through the window. I thank God for sunlight because it allows me to see every blessed, beautiful inch of him without the need to rush.

"What's wrong? Why'd you stop?" I ask.

"Nothin'." He wraps an arm around my legs and pulls me flat along the bed. Then he spreads out alongside me, tucking my body into his.

"What are you doing?"

"Shhh." He presses a finger to my lips. "I want to touch you. I wanna make you forget everything. I wanna make you feel better. Will you let me?"

My breath hitches in my chest and I can only nod. His finger traces my bottom lip, his eyes captivated by the movement. I'm trembling by the time his mouth comes back to mine. I can feel his smile against my lips. He has me right where he wants me and he damn well knows it.

His hand glides over the material of my bra underneath my hospital gown, so close to the aching weight of my breasts.

I make a frustrated noise and he laughs, diverting his hand to the exposed skin of my knees. Even better.

The tips of his fingernails scrape along the skin of my thighs and at this point, I've virtually given up on ever breathing again. He makes one painstaking journey up to the top of my thigh, then stops and changes direction.

I grab on to his shoulder, discarding any rational thought, and press against him. "Please," I whisper.

Our eyes lock and his hand presses against where I need him the most. I can feel the heat of him through the thin material and my eyes drift closed at the overwhelming sensation.

I feel him dip his head next to my ear and he says, "No, baby, I want to see your eyes."

I bite my tongue and do as he says. He rewards me with the gentle play of his fingers, ever so soft, against me. And oh, God, the feeling is amplified a hundred times because it's nowhere near as hard as I need it. No, instead, he traces me in small, languid circles until my hips are matching the back and forth movement of his hand.

My cheeks burn hot with shame and want. I shouldn't be doing this. He slips his devilish fingers underneath the material of my panties and all good sense escapes me. My entire body bows up in response, muscles arched in a sweet ache of unleashed tension.

"You like that, Chloe?" His voice. God that voice. Each whisper sends a shockwave along my body, inciting the heat growing in my core as though it were a caress. He'll devastate every one of my senses before this is over, I swear.

"Please," I whisper.

"You want it?" he grunts.

I hold my breath in my chest like a captive trying to force myself over the peak. My hips roll against the soft play of his fingers and each flutter brings me ever closer to relief.

"Yes," I hiss as he speeds up. "Yes, just like that."

His fingers move lower and I let out a sobbing breath. *Yes, yes, yes,* I think to myself. His chuckle is a rumble in my ear.

Then, disaster strikes and three things happen all at once. First, he plunges two fingers deep inside of me, and I come. Exquisitely. Deliciously. Fantastically hard. Then, the door to his hospital room bursts open.

CHAPTER THIRTEEN

GABRIEL

I'VE NOT BEEN a man prone to violence in my personal life. Temper, maybe. Do I have a tendency to be a jerk at times? Sure, if the situation warrants it. But never in my life have I wanted to throttle someone quite as much as I do in this moment.

The rapturous expression on Chloe's face, the one that I was admiring mere moments before, is replaced by panic and I instinctively move to cover her half-exposed body with my own. I, regretfully, free my hand to grab the blankets and pull them over us. Beneath me, she's trembling and I let loose a string of expletives.

"Shit," Tyler says and then covers his twinkling eyes, the bastard. "Didn't think you'd have company."

I'm going to kill him. I'll be sad to see him go, but it must be done.

"Bit busy here, Ty," I bite out.

Tyler, damn him to hell, grins and says, "I'll say."

Maybe I'll enjoy killing him. "Get your ass out of here before I throw you out, man."

With his hands still covering his eyes he says, "Nice to meet you, Ms. McKinney."

Her face a gorgeous color of red, Chloe peers out from behind the blanket and says, "Nice to meet you, too."

"My name's Tyler. The idiot you're with is a good friend of mine. I was going to find out which hotel room you were in, but this saves me the trouble."

"Ty!" I shout. "Wrap it up."

"Just wanted to tell you thanks for taking care of our guy," he says.

Chloe smiles even though he can't see her. "You're welcome," she says. "It's nice to meet you, officially."

"Why don't you have Gabe bring you over next weekend? My wife and I are going to grill out." Before she can respond, Tyler gropes for the handle of the door. "I won't take no for an answer now," he says. "So I expect to see you on Saturday. You two have fun."

He makes a quick escape before I can untangle myself from Chloe's arms and the grasping tangle of the monitor wires.

She puts a hand on my shoulder and I still. "It's okay," she says softly.

I fight my way out of the wires until I can see her face.

"Are you sure? I never should have—I mean I should have waited."

Her hand moves up my cheek. "No, it's okay. It was pretty damn good actually."

Her shy confession makes me want to do it all over again. "Really?" I ask, my voice husky.

"Really."

I kiss her again, because I can. When it ends, she rests her head on my chest and draws patterns on my stomach. "When do you have to go home?" I almost don't want to know the answer, but I figure I'd better rip off the band aid.

She shrugs. "I'm not sure. My boss, her name's Sienna, we've been good friends for a long time. Anyway, she feels like shit for making me get on that ferry so I think it's safe to assume I'll have as much vacation time as I want for the foreseeable future."

"This Sienna sounds like a great friend."

"She is. Anyway, why'd you want to know?" she teases. "Want me out of here?"

"Definitely not." I hesitate, then barrel through. "I'm asking 'cause I was going to see if you wanted to come stay at my place. I mean until you have to go back."

We knock heads when she arches backward to look at me. "Are you sure?" she asks. "What about Emily? I wouldn't want to intrude."

"She's with her mom. They both hadn't slept in a couple days and Emily was getting a little cranky. She's so young, I didn't want to scare her being at the hospital so much. They're staying at her mom's house for a couple days and then Em's gonna come spend the week with me when things calm down. I don't want you to feel obligated—"

"Yes," she says.

"Yeah?"

Laughter spills from her lips. "I said yes. When do we get out of here?"

"If they don't let me out by this afternoon, we'll break out."

"Bonnie and Clyde style," she jokes, then she grows serious. "Have you heard anything about the others? I mean the other hostages. The captain."

I sigh and pull her closer against me like I can shield her from everything. The fact that I even want to does not bode well for my dedicated bachelorhood, but I set that aside.

"There were some injuries, a couple serious, but everyone is expected to recover. They haven't found the captain yet." I swallow thickly. "They've sent out Search & Rescue, but no luck yet."

"I'm so sorry, Gabe," she says.

"Me, too."

"It's not your fault though, you know that, right?" When I don't answer, she looks up at me. "Right?" she insists.

I sigh. "Intellectually, yes, I know that, but emotionally, I feel every single death like a chain around my neck. On some level, if I had saved her, none of this would have happened."

"Oh, honey," she whispers and then kisses my throat. "You can't control everything."

"Chloe, I'm a man. I have to think that I can or I'll self-destruct." I joke, but a part of me is serious.

"You're not God, it's not like you can influence other people's decisions or control the weather."

Not wanting to talk about it anymore, I crowd her on the small bed. "Sure about that?" I caress her arm with the pads of my fingers. "Pretty sure I can *influence* you."

She slaps my hand away. "Don't try and change the subject."

Irritation makes my response curt. "Look, I'm into you, but I don't want to talk about this right now. It'll work itself out eventually. Can't we go back to how it was before we brought that shit up?"

The hurt on her face makes my gut ache, but I don't take it back. Her throat bobs with a swallow and she forces a smile. "Sure, you're right. I shouldn't press the issue. I'm sorry."

My smile is tight. "Forget about it," I say.

A tense silence descends until she breaks it by clearing her throat. "I think, uh, I'd better get back to my room before they send out a search party for me." She eases herself off the bed, careful not to bump my injuries and straightens her hospital gown self-consciously. When she's done, she glances up. "I'll see you later?" she asks over her shoulder as she walks to the door and pauses.

I nod and she slips out the door.

Good job, Gabe.

Growling, I throw a pillow at the wall and cover my eyes

with my arm. I hope I didn't screw us up before we'd even really gotten started.

CHLOE

Five o'clock rolls around and I sit on my bed watching the seconds tick by and cursing myself for my stupidity. I knew I shouldn't have gone to him. I shouldn't have made myself vulnerable like that.

Gabe's been radio silent since I left his room this morning. If he doesn't come in the next few minutes, I'll get a hotel room for the night—at least until my parent's drive in. I won't feel safe at my house all alone. For the foreseeable future, I want to surround myself with people to combat the feeling I'm being watched.

Which is silly. I've been in a hospital surrounded by orderlies and nurses and doctors coming in and out of the room checking on my arm and running countless tests. Not including the barrage of journalists who try to sneak past the cops guarding the floor or the other survivors who've been coming by in a constant stream to give their thanks.

With all the attention, of course I feel like all eyes are on me. It'll take a couple days for all of the attention to die down and for things to go back to normal. Then this itchy feeling will go away and I'll be able to relax.

One minute left.

The doorknob wiggles and I glance up to find Gabe pushing his way through.

He pauses in the doorway, and I take the moment to study him. His firm jawline is set and his mouth is pressed into a line. His unreadable green eyes are on me and I feel them like a flash of heat.

"I'm sorry," he says before I can even open my mouth. "I was a dick."

"You weren't," I say, but he shakes his head.

"No, I know when I'm being a dick and I'm man enough to apologize for it. It's a sensitive subject right now."

"I know; I shouldn't have pressed the issue. I still want to go with you, if you're up for it."

I barely finish the sentence when he's pulling me up from the bed and whirling me around. I have the instinctual urge to flee, but he is like gravity and I don't have the strength to resist his pull.

Nor do I have the strength to resist his kiss.

His lips slant across mine as he pins me against the wall with his rock hard body. My hands go up to grip his nape because the mere taste of him is enough to knock me off my feet. I make an involuntary surprised sound against the potent press of his lips.

His hands slide down my neck to the curve of my arm, and then traverse the length of my back. He reaches the flare of my hips and his fingers flex against the material of my clothes, gripping my hip, pressing me against the thick length of his arousal.

I may be tall for a woman, but Gabe towers over me. His massive shoulders and arms surround me until I'm helpless against him. His lips play over mine, again and again, until he coaxes my mouth to open for him.

With that, he makes a growling sound deep in his throat and hitches my leg up and around his hip, causing the thin material of the borrowed dress Sienna gave me to spread until I'm bare against him. Then I'm overcome by the wet sound of our lips, the gasping breaths I'm able to take in between, and the little rumbles of satisfaction he makes in the back of his throat.

My hair tumbles from the sloppy bun I'd thrown it up in after my shower, and falls in a wet mass of tangles over my shoulders. It surrounds us in the soft scent of coconut and vanilla, and he breaks the kiss to press his face into the curve of my shoulder. He inhales there, nuzzling my skin with the sandpaper-scratch of his beard. It tickles every nerve ending I possess until I become one live wire from head to toe.

"I had to see you again," he confesses, his voice a mere whisper against my neck. The confession washes away everything else until the only things left are me and him.

My arms twitch around his shoulders and I pull him closer, almost afraid that if I let go, he'll evaporate and this will all have been a dream. "I'm sorry I upset you."

He laughs, his hands running lines up and down my back, pressing into the muscles and soothing me into a stupor. "Don't be sorry, it's my fault."

I make a sound and try to pull back, but he doesn't let me.

He pulls me closer, hands still massaging my back and lulling me into complacency. "No, don't pull away. I like how you feel against me." He presses a kiss to my hair and I remember that he did the same thing when we were on the ferry. "I was perfectly content to go on living my life as I had been. And then you crashed in and changed all of my plans. What are you doing to me?" he whispers.

I stretch up to nibble his ear. "Anything you want," I reply.

He chuckles, and the sound warms me from the inside out. "We don't have much time to waste and I want to spend it getting to know you more. So, I know we've done this backward, considering we've already essentially slept together. But, Chloe McKinney..." he pauses for one long heartbeat, making my breath catch in my throat. "Would you like to have dinner? Officially?"

My heart nearly explodes with joy and I smile so huge that my cheeks hurt. It's like a dream. I can't stop the laughter that escapes. I press my lips to his. And it's sloppy and crazy, but we're both smiling when we break apart, and on him, God, it's beautiful. A heart-stopping kind of beautiful.

I peer up at him. "Will you take offense if I say I'm not up for being seen in public just yet?"

"Don't worry. I know the perfect place and it's very private. What do you say?"

"I trust you," I whisper.

He backs away with careful steps, like he doesn't want to leave either, and I scoot past him. I can feel his eyes following my every movement as I grab clothes from the suitcase I'd already packed up, and head to the bathroom to change.

The only clean outfit I have that's good enough for an actual date is a ridiculously sexy shift dress that Sienna insisted I take "just in case." Nerves wage war in my stomach as I slip into it. It flows loosely around my thighs and the arms are long sleeved with slits from shoulder to wrist. The slight tan I have looks phenomenal. My hair can't be helped, so I brush it out and plait it into a simple braid I let hang over my shoulder.

I don't bother with any makeup, aside from a little mascara and gloss. He's already seen me at my worst anyway, and he still wants me. Something about that makes me ridiculously happy.

I give myself one last cursory glance in the mirror and then slip on my sandals. Gabriel is standing by the window looking out at the view. I pad across the room and wrap my arms around his waist. His hands cover mine and he gives me a gentle squeeze. He taps them and I release my hold.

"All ready to go?" He turns and gives me a once over. "You look amazing."

"Thank you. Are you going to tell me where we're going?"

"This great Italian place I know. Trust me, you're gonna love it."

CHAPTER FOURTEEN

GABRIEL

"You're the whole package, aren't you? Sexy, smart, and now you say you can cook? My hero." Chloe bats her eyes and settles onto a stool, leaning on my island bar. She crosses her legs and I have to fight not to stare at her. Wisps of hair have broken free of her loose braid to frame her face. She looks good in my house. Like she belongs here.

"A man can't give away all his secrets, now, can he?" I pause while dicing tomatoes to kiss her soft lips, and then once more for good measure. Responding immediately, her hands slide up to my neck and I almost say to hell with dinner.

I'd forgotten how nice it was to cook for someone other than myself. Chloe spent the last ten minutes entertaining me with stories about the antics of her family and the crazy clients she's had at the travel agency she helps manage.

"Well, none of the men in my family have ever been able

to make more than scrambled eggs. I've never wanted a plate of spaghetti more in my life after all the hospital food. Seriously, it smells amazing."

"Of course it does. Plus, this serves dual purposes. It's both dinner and a seduction."

Chloe's eyes light up. "Oh, is it?" she murmurs.

"You bet. Cooking for a woman is my best move." I pour the diced tomatoes into the sauce and stir, glancing at her over the steaming pot.

She sets her glass down on the counter and snuggles into my side. "Oh, so this is something you do for all the ladies, huh?"

"Only the special ones."

"I bet you save all of them, too." She jabs me in my uninjured ribs and I laugh. "Is there anything I can help you with?"

"No, you don't worry about it. I'm going to take care of you tonight." And I mean that in more ways than one, if she'll let me.

She brushes off my statement and moves to root through my fridge. "Aha," she exclaims. I turn to find her with arms full of salad mixings. She dumps the supplies on the counter and then turns to search in the cabinets.

"What are you doing?" She bumps her head on the open cabinet and yelps.

"You okay?"

"I'm seeing double, but at least I found a salad bowl."

I tug on her free hand and circle her in my arms. "I told you that you didn't have to help."

"It's just a bump. I'll be fine."

I grab a cloth and some ice from the dispenser and press it to the goose egg already swelling on her head. "You sit and relax. If you must do something, you can put together that salad while sitting. Surely, you can't get hurt that way," I tease. "The last thing we need is to take you back to the hospital."

"Har, har." She gets to work shredding and assembling the salad. "So I'm a little clumsy. You should probably know that about me up front. I also do crazy things like challenge people with guns. Spend the night with a strange man."

"Do that often?"

She sputters around a sip of her drink. "Completely not what I meant and you know it."

"C'mon. You're gorgeous. I wouldn't hold it against you even if you had. But you also don't seem like the kind of girl to take relationships lightly."

"Got me there. The last one I had ended pretty badly."

"What happened?"

"Well, he told me he couldn't ruin our friendship in case something went wrong with our relationship. He was my best friend when we got together." She drinks heartily. "Did I mention he was my fiancé when he dumped me and he recently got engaged? Again."

"His loss," I tell her. And I'm being serious, even if she doesn't think so. Only an idiot would let a woman like Chloe slip through their fingers, and I'm not a fuckin' idiot.

"You're so sweet." She finishes sprinkling cheese on the salad and wipes her hands on a cloth. Finished, she scoots off the stool and rewraps her hand around my waist. She smells candy-sweet. Too sweet for an asshole like me, that's for damn sure, but hell if I'm gonna let her go. I find the source of the scent at the base of her neck and nibble there.

"You didn't think that a few days ago," I mumble into her throat. "In fact, if I remember correctly, you weren't very nice."

"Well, I didn't know you a few days ago."

I bend her over the counter as my lips find her mouth. "I think you need to get to know me even better," I say against her lips.

Chloe

"I don't know about this."

Gabriel smiles devilishly and I respond with a full body shiver. Now that I know he wants me in return, it's like I have no control over my reactions to him.

We'd spent the last hour talking about everything. And I mean everything. He told me about his years in the Marines, and how much he wanted to get away from his horrible home life to make something out of himself.

I learned that he was one of those rare unicorns who believed in love and marriage, and when his had turned sour, it ruined him for future relationships. I'm not normally one to speak ill of another, but his wife has to be out of her mind to give up a great man like Gabe. Then again if she hadn't, we never would have met.

Once he finally lets his guard down, he is truly a thing of beauty. His smile—and his *damn good* spaghetti—had me reduced to a pile of goo by the time dinner was over. Well, that and the two drinks I've had to celebrate.

I toss my napkin onto the table with a groan. "I can't possibly eat any more."

"Excellent. Time for the next surprise."

The food coma I'm nursing abates a little. "Next surprise?" I eye him warily. "If it's dessert, I hate to say it, but I'm seriously going to have to pass. There's no way."

He chuckles and takes our dishes to the kitchen to rinse. While sitting back and relaxing, I hear a whine coming from outside, so I go out to the porch to investigate. I open the sliding glass door and am attacked by a blur of black and white. I immediately crouch down and start loving on the dog —a Boston Terrier from the looks of it. He's equal parts bug eyes and smashed nose and the most awesome combination of ugly and cute.

"Who is this guy?"

"That's Rudy. I'm surprised he didn't introduce himself earlier."

Rudy jumps up and licks all over my face. "Well, he's definitely affectionate." I laugh and give him a good back scratch. None of my apartments have allowed pets, and I've wanted one for years. "I bet he and Emily are best buddies."

"Oh, they are. He ditches me to sleep in her room whenever she visits."

"Was he my surprise?"

"This handsome guy? Unfortunately, no. But I'm sure he's loving the attention." Rudy pants happily, rolling over on his back so I can give his belly a scratch, too.

We leave him a sated mess on the porch and Gabriel leads me down the steps and to a walkway. He situates me in front of him and covers my eyes with his hands and we walk in tandem through a gathering of trees behind his house. We stop and Gabe presses against my back, breath tickling my ear as he says, "Keep your eyes closed. No peeking."

"Is this one of those situations where I should be running for my life?"

"If you run, I'll just have to catch you."

He leads me down a concrete path. I can hear the waves in the distance. After a while the concrete gives way to dirt and I have to squeeze my eyes together to keep from peeking. The sound of waves grows louder the longer we walk and then he brings us to a stop. My feet sink into the sand as my breath shortens.

"Open your eyes."

I take a few useless breaths, which do nothing to calm the internal freak out that's going on inside of me, and do as he says. He drops my hand and as soon as my eyes open he brings his fingers to his top button and undoes his shirt.

And oh, God, I go weak in the knees. I see the most magnificent expanse of chest, and sweet baby Jesus, I swear I see a flash of happy trail as he reaches the bottom. His abs flex as he strips it off the rest of the way and drops it by his feet.

He's going to kill me.

A few seconds later, he leads me to a spot in the sand where he spreads out a blanket I didn't even notice he was carrying. Then he holds out his hand for mine and when I take it he guides me down to the blanket.

He watches with hooded eyes as I recline next to him and slip off my sandals. The cool air bathes my skin, though it does little to cool the heat inside me. My hands grip the material because the sight of him sends a rush of intense arousal through me.

Gabe shifts toward me, his easy-going mood replaced by desire. When I shift again, he surrounds me with his arms and I melt against him.

The cocoon he's created with the waves and the heat from his body heighten every sensation—the smooth feeling of his skin rubbing against mine, the gentle tug of the wind running through my hair. Even though he's barely touching me at all, he's turned me on more than I've ever been in my life. This morning included.

Then he moves to me, pressing me against the blanket, his arms a cage I never want to leave. His arousal presses thick and hot against the thin material of my panties. My legs go up and around his hips to urge him closer, the way I've been wanting to all day.

His hands tangle in my hair and he pulls back just enough that my body is hovering on the precipice of pleasure and pain. With little bites, he trails a line down my throat to the thin material covering my breasts. He covers one nipple with an open-mouthed kiss, taking it between his teeth. The twin bites of pain, which are so good it hurts, cause me to cry out.

"Yes," he whispers against my skin. "I want to hear you come for me this time. No one here but you and me and I'm gonna make you scream."

He bites, nips, and kisses his way to my other breast. This time, he pulls down the material of my bra to use his teeth and tongue to drive me to distraction. I clasp his head and writhe against him. My hips move in subtle motions that mimic the flicks of his tongue. I arch into him, giving him everything. I'd only managed a taste of how good it would be between us before, and it was even better the second time around.

His hands drift down my sides and grip my thighs. For one glorious moment, his cock is right where I need it. I throw my head back in response. He uses his hands to glide my pussy up and down the length of him, taking care not to hinder his attention to my breasts.

"You feel so good." His voice is hoarse and he rests his head between my breasts as he attempts to catch his breath.

"So do you."

He lifts his eyes to mine and now it's nothing but the gentle rhythm of us rocking against each other. My hands map their way over his sun-browned shoulders and down his sculpted chest. I pause to flick the rigid tips of his nipples and delight in the strangled groan it elicits from his throat. He's covered in a smattering of scars and I want to trace every one of them with my mouth and tongue.

I lean back to get a look at his face so I can commit it to

memory. He follows curving his body toward mine. His hands have my hips in an immovable grip as though he's afraid I'll somehow slip out of his grasp.

But he doesn't have to worry.

I'm not going anywhere.

CHAPTER FIFTEEN

GABRIEL

THE SLICK PRESS of her skin and her short little pants and whimpers of pleasure will haunt me for a lifetime. She tastes sweet and salty, and I can't stop kissing her, sampling her everywhere I can reach.

When she untangles her legs to pay my body the same attention, my stomach contracts in pleasure. Her hands slide down my chest and her nails rake my abs. My breath catches in my throat when her hand clasps around me and strokes between us. When my head drops to her shoulder, I bite the skin there as my hips thrust my cock into her palm.

I cup her jaw and I look into her eyes. "I want you, Chloe. Now."

She squeezes around me, pumping once, slowly. Torturously. "Yes," is all she can manage to say.

And that's all I need.

I roll onto my back, in deference to my injuries, and put my hands on her waist. She squeals as I lift her by her hips and arrange her legs on either side of my head.

As much as I enjoy her hands on me, it feels like I've been waiting an eternity to taste her. I push up the material of her dress, inch by inch as she's watching me with heavily lidded eyes and sucking on her lower lip until its red and glistening.

I groan at the sight and slide my hands up the long length of her legs. She shivers and my lips curve up in a smile. It's been so long since I've been able to take the time to enjoy sex with someone who won't be leaving as soon as the sun comes up.

Watching her little responses to my every touch is a hell of a turn on. My fingers tease at the sensitive skin on the back of her knees and then scrape a line down her inner thighs. Her breathing shallows the closer I get and so does mine.

Her panties are see-through by this point. The shadow of her pussy and the small strip of hair are unmistakable. I trace the line with the soft touch of my finger from top to bottom. Her hips follow the movement and a hopeless mewl comes from her throat. With one hand, I pull her panties to the side and use the thumb of the other to start a gentle rhythm against her clit. I watch as her eyes drift closed and then I arch up and press my mouth right to that spot.

Her body tightens around me and she leans forward to cup the back of my head with both hands. She murmurs encouragements, pleads to deities and lets loose a string of obscenities, but I don't stop. I'm mindless with the sharp taste of her arousal.

Her pleas devolve into babbling. I watch as her eyes flash open and she pushes up to watch me work her. The sight of me between her legs drives her body wild. Her knees find purchase on the sand and she uses that to add weight behind her hips, meeting me in an imitation of sex as my tongue spears into her.

Her breath comes out in short sobs. Her knees squeeze my head, and her moans surround us both. I release my grip on her thighs as she melts. Her chest heaves and her entire body seizes. I watch as she stutters through her orgasm, a blush blooming over her chest and cheeks and then her body goes limp.

It was worth the wait.

CHLOE

It takes a few more moments before my hearing returns. Then I remember that I have eyes that do a beautiful thing called seeing, so I open them for a test drive to see if they're still working. The first thing I see is Gabe pressing kisses against my thighs, thighs that are still trembling from the most intense orgasm of my life. Somehow, he maneuvers me back down to the blanket.

"Baby," he whispers, running a thumb along my lower lip. The thought makes me smile. "You okay?"

I make a sound that doesn't seem intelligible, but he soothes me with a hand on my hair.

My head lolls against his shoulder, and for a moment, I'm content to feel him against me and soothe me back down.

He lets me relax against him as feeling returns to my limbs and the slight ringing fades from my ears. As the numbness begins to dissipate, I become aware of his rock hard body against my own. The insatiable need he has stoked inside of me returns, making me stir against him.

He has me pinned, again, against the blanket with my arms wrapped around his shoulders. If I weren't on fire with the need to have him inside me, I would be satisfied to rest here for a year or two—it is *that* comfortable. I use my grip on his neck to bring his mouth to mine.

When our lips touch, I sigh into the contact. I swear this man can kiss. It's shameful how his lips and tongue conquer my mouth, how I don't give a second thought to giving up all control. He has this way of enveloping me with his body and making me feel powerful and vulnerable all at once. And it occurs to me that this feeling is a lot like love.

The need to get ever closer consumes me until I crawl up his body, forgetting that I'm still wearing panties. Gabriel reaches down and with a sharp tug, divests me of that barrier. His hands go around me and he undoes the bra's clasp. I tug it off my arms and toss it behind me. His cock rubs against my sensitized clit with gentle thrusts from his hips. Each time the tip brushes against me, a little sound erupts from my chest.

I lean backward against the blanket, his arms cradling me. The angle shifts and he hunkers down around me, his eyes blazing. He continues the gentle back and forth, his cock cradled between the lips of my pussy and pressed against my clit, in a way that makes me see stars.

But this time, I need more. I disengage, angling my hips so that his next thrust presses against my entrance. His shoulders lock under my hands and choke on a swift surprised inhalation.

"God, that feels so good."

"So good," he agrees.

His face distorts and I peer up at him. "What's wrong?"

"Condom," he chokes out. "I'm clean, regular checks."

"Me, too."

"I need to have you on a bed. My bed."

My body wants him anywhere I can have him, but I agree. He lifts me from the blanket and we both dress quickly. Mindlessly, I follow him back up to the house, through the kitchen where the scent of our meal still lingers and then, finally, into a darkened bedroom.

I'm covered in gooseflesh from the cool air and when he turns to lay his hands on my shoulders, I shiver. We both climb on the bed and I curl up to him as he wraps the covers around us both.

"We don't have to do this right away," he mumbles into my hair. "If it's too soon, we can wait."

"You would wait?'

"Not happily, but I would."

"That's sweet." I nip at his lips. "But completely unnecessary."

And then I dive under the covers.

CHAPTER SIXTEEN

GABRIEL

SHE LICKS DOWN the skin of my abdomen, pausing to bite my hip. My hands clutch by my sides so that I don't grip her hair to move her mouth exactly where I want it. When she nuzzles my groin, her cheek brushing against my cock, I tug on the covers, pulling them up so I can watch her work between my legs. The sight is almost more than I can handle.

Her dark hair is falling around her naked shoulders. She needs to be naked like this all day, every day. As wet heat surrounds the head of my cock, I make a promise to myself that I will do everything in my power to convince this woman never to leave.

"Yes..." I hiss.

Her eyes peer up and I'm entranced by the glide of her mouth over me. She grips the base and my hands lift to guide her head. Not with force, more as an encouragement, because, honestly, there is nothing she could possibly do to drive me even more out of my mind.

As she catches a rhythm, I lift my hips to match her movements. The gentle flicks of her tongue and the soft suction of her lips increase and her eyes flutter closed. Her obvious enjoyment turns me on as much as the erotic sounds coming from her chest. My abdomen tightens and I thrust one, two, three times before I pull back. It feels too good.

"Stop, stop, stop."

Her mouth slicks up one more time and releases with a pop. She smiles and leans over me, her body now warm and pliant against mine. I capture her lips with mine and grab her generous ass, molding and shaping it at my whim. She rubs up against me like a cat and takes my earlobe between her teeth. Heat streaks through me and I fumble with my side table for a condom.

My breath stutters through my lips and I fumble putting it on. Her fingers reach back and take my length in her hands. She arches up, breasts tipped in a rosy pink so delectable that I take one into my mouth for a taste as she lowers herself down onto my length.

Normally, I need to be in control, but with my leg, I doubt I'll be able to do any missionary anytime soon. I change my mind as soon as her heat slicks over me. Girl on top is my new favorite position. We groan in unison and she arches her back, her hands coming to my shoulders to balance her weight.

Her hair falls in a cascade around us as she looks down to watch her pussy taking me. The tight grip of her velvet heat is so much better than I'd imagined. She bottoms out, her ass resting on my legs and I'm seated deep inside her. Her tongue comes out to lick a line around her lips and I want to taste that, too. I capture her mouth with mine and use my hands to lift her hips.

"I've never," she mumbles against my lips, her breath coming in sobs. "God, it's never felt so good. I want you so much, but I don't want to hurt you."

"The only way you're gonna hurt me is if you stop," I say.

I tease her with a drag of my cock against her soft folds and she squirms against me. It's never been a big thing of mine to watch a woman getting off. But after seeing her face this morning, the only thing I could think about all day was doing it again.

"Don't make me get my handcuffs, Gabe," she practically snarls after a few long, tortuous minutes of teasing. "Fuck me."

I laugh darkly and then thrust into her. She bares her throat to me and I latch onto her neck as I grind into her. She reaches a hand down to where we're joined and my eyes follow the movement of her hand as she fingers my cock driving into her. I love that so much, I almost come from that alone. She brings her fingers back up to squeeze and roll her nipples.

"That's so fucking hot," I growl. "So fucking sweet. I want to watch you."

Her cheeks flush and she blinks down at me. For a second, I think she's going to balk and then she grasps my head in her hands and guides me to her breasts that are still shiny with her arousal. I tongue a nipple, tasting a combination of her and the salt of sweat.

I glide in and out of her, adjusting her legs so that they are spread wide, and the sight of her is so goddamn explicit I groan just looking at her.

I must hit some crazy good spot because her walls clamp down around me with each thrust and she goes statue-still. Noting her response, I shorten my thrusts until I'm working that spot with each movement. Her arms constrict around me and she alternatively pushes me and pulls me closer.

"Gabe, what are you do-ohmiGod. Gabriel, please."

I nuzzle her throat and put my mouth to her ear. "I told you I was gonna make you scream."

She glares at me around a moan and I resist the urge to smirk in response. It's all bravado, though, because she's so fuckin' tight around me now that I'm about to come, myself. I wedge a finger between us to flick against her now sensitive clit. It doesn't take much for her to clamp around me with a keening wail. Her nails dig into my back and I work her through the aftershocks of her orgasm with soft, slow movements.

I almost consider working her over the edge one more time, before the past twenty-four hours of foreplay grab me by the balls and I tumble right after her.

CHLOE

My arms wrap around his wide shoulders. His solidity anchors me in the moment and I soak it all up like it'll be our last. Our bodies are a slick mess and the scent of him is all over my skin. I rock my hips against his and he mumbles something against my shoulder.

"Wanna take a shower with me?"

He lifts up enough to peer at me contemplatively. "As long as you wash my back."

I laugh. "Deal."

We untangle ourselves from his sheets and stumble blindly into the bathroom. The water heats and then we shift under the spray, expressing twin moans of delight as the hot water beats down upon us. I gather his body wash and squeeze some on a loofah. As I scrub his back, I giggle at the fact that this badass man has a loofah in his shower. He can cook and he takes care of himself. The twinge between my legs reminds me that he can also take damn good care of me.

I trace the lines of his body absently as I consider that thought. We hadn't talked about where the attraction between us was leading. Now that we've had sex, what else is there left to say? I have a job, a life to get back to. He has his life here. Neither of us have mentioned anything long term and isn't that the number one thing you don't do with a man? Smother him?

Especially after what we've been through.

Gabriel turns in my arms, but I'm not able to look him

directly in the eye for fear that I'll give my thoughts away. Even if this is a one-time thing, it's the best thing to happen to me in a long time. I don't want to ruin it by forcing seriousness into the situation too early.

I busy myself with thoroughly washing his chest. I ditch the loofah to pay homage with my hands. There are some things that I can't resist, and a set of powerful shoulders and a non-manscaped chest are two of them. My fingers spread suds over his light dusting of hair and I play with the trail leading down to his cock. He makes a strangled sound in response and I grin inwardly.

"What are you thinking so hard about?" he asks gruffly.

"Hmm?"

"You've got that crease between your eyes. I've noticed it means you're thinking hard about something. To be honest, it kind of pisses me off—if I had the energy to be pissed off that is."

I smile up at him. "You're always pissed off."

He slaps my ass and I squeak. "I am not. I just have a low tolerance for bullshit. In any case, don't try to distract me. The fact that you even have energy leftover tells me that maybe I didn't do a good enough job. Do I need to give you something else to think about?"

His fingers glide up my thigh and he plunges two inside of me. I'm so sensitive that their soft intrusion has my vision flashing to white.

"Now I've got your attention," he murmurs, slowly fingering me into complacency, "tell me what's wrong?"

"N-nothing!" I gasp as his fingers surge inside of me.

It takes no time at all for my body to shake with an impending orgasm. I grip his shoulders and roll my hips in an effort to bring me to the edge.

But instead of going faster, harder, his fingers retreat and he touches my folds softly, delicately, and asks me again, "What's wrong? And don't lie to me."

"I was thinking about how sad I'm going to be when I have to go home."

He cups my cheeks in his hands. "I'm going to miss you, too," is all he says.

Then he pins me against the wall and there is something about being near helpless and vulnerable to him that makes me come harder than I ever have in my life. It's not until I'm near sleep twenty minutes later, wrapped up in his arms, that I realize he never gave me any assurances one way or the other.

CHAPTER SEVENTEEN

GABRIEL

"Gabe?"

I shake my head and snuggle back into the pillow, trying to drift back to sleep. The combination of exhaustion, stress, and sex is a potent one and I'm going to need a week of sleep to recover.

"Gabe, Rudy's barking," Chloe grumbles.

"He'll be fine," I say.

For a few minutes I drift back to sleep and then Rudy starts barking again and this time it sounds like he's trying to claw his way through the door. With a curse, I throw the covers off of my legs and reach blindly for a pair of sweats that are, generally, always on the floor beside my bed. I slip them on and stumble for the bedroom door.

I find Rudy outside my bedroom and glare at him. "Next

time I'm going to lock you up in a cage when we go to bed," I tell him.

He pants happily as we walk through the dark hallway to the patio door. I yawn as I yank it open to let him out and he races across the lawn to his favorite bushes.

While he's doing his business, I figure I might as well get something to drink because the marathon sex gave me a powerful thirst. As I make myself a glass of ice water, I consider how to play the morning after, so to speak.

It's probably too early to start talking commitments and considering both of our romantic histories, one of us is likely to balk if we start moving too quickly. The best option is for us to take this slowly. Hell, that's probably what people call dating. The thought makes me frown, but fuck it. If that's what I have to do to keep her coming back, I will.

I drain the glass of water and immediately make another. I chug that one as well and by that time, Rudy's done outside and is scratching to come back in.

"You're lucky you're cute," I tell him as I close the door behind him.

When I look up, I catch a movement in the glass and I only have a few seconds to duck before the gun the man is holding discharges and a bullet shatters the glass. My leg screams in pain as I crouch down and glass rains down around me.

"Get up," the man shouts.

"I'm about fucking sick of people pointing guns in my

face," I say as I get to my feet. I feel wetness on my thigh and my feet are probably sliced to hell, but I'm done.

The man flicks on the dining room light where the dishes from our dinner still sit and I nearly fall backward when I realize who the man is.

It's the captain. The one no one's been able to find since Jones threw him overboard that night. He sure doesn't look dead.

"What the hell are you doing here?" I ask, trying, and failing to keep my voice level.

"I'm here to finish what that idiot couldn't."

"Finish…" I trail off. "What are you talking about?"

"He never was good enough for my daughter," he says.

"Daughter?" I repeat numbly. "Your daughter."

"Shelia," he says. "He never appreciated her, but man, I never thought he was stupid as well as useless."

My brain, still hazy with sleep, takes a second to piece things together. When I do, my first thought is of Chloe, who's still in the other room. If she isn't awake by now, it'd be a miracle.

"You're—"

"That's right. Sheila's father. Phillip Langford."

"We saved you," I say.

Phillip spits on the floor by my feet. "You ruined me. My daughter is dead because of you."

I shake my head, but the images of Samuel Jones and his wife, both still, so goddamned still, surface in my brain, distracting me even as the gun twitches in Phillip's hand.

"I never meant for anyone to get hurt," I tell him. I start to back up into the backyard. I don't even feel it as the shards of glass bite into the soft soles of my feet.

"I give a fuck for your intentions. Now shut the fuck up and get that bitch out here, too."

I make it across the doorway and take the first step onto the back porch. He jerks the gun at me.

"Don't take another step," he says as he moves toward me, "or I'll fucking shoot you right now."

"I won't let you hurt her," I tell him.

He takes a step closer. "Too bad," he says.

Then he jerks forward with a sound of surprise and I find Chloe behind him, with a bat she must have found in my closet, poised over him.

"Are you okay?" she asks breathlessly.

CHLOE

"I don't think we can see each other anymore," I tell Gabe once the furor dies down.

He looks at me, too exhausted to react. "Why's that?"

"Your life is much too exciting for me," I say emphatically.

Laughter dances in his eyes, even though he can barely keep his head up. "That so?"

Somehow, our hands find each other. I don't know if it was a conscious decision on our part, or if we've somehow forged a link through tragedy that can never be broken. Either way, I don't want to let go.

"Yes," I say, once I manage to find the words. "I think I'm over the excitement. After this, only boring dates from now on."

Gabe grunts as he shoulders through the paramedics working on him to sit beside me in the ambulance. Red and blue lights play over his face. "So this *was* a date?"

I chew on my bottom lip and look down at my feet. Shit, was I wrong? Was this too soon? I knew I should have kept things casual. I shake my head mentally. I never learn. After Thomas, you think I'd be a pro at knowing when a man wants to ditch me.

He thumbs my chin up. "I don't know if I could call this a date," he says. When I start to pull away he holds me captive. "What I feel for you goes past the normal get-to-know-you stage, Chloe. I don't have a name for it, but I do know I want to see you again. I don't want this to end."

My spine straightens and I wrap my uninjured arm around my waist to contain the urge to jump up and tackle him. "You don't?"

Gabe shakes his head and his hand slides down to cup my cheek. I find myself leaning into his touch despite my better judgment.

"Of course not."

"But what about—"

He kisses me and then leans his forehead against mine. There are paramedics, policemen, and even F.B.I agents darting around us. It's chaos, but when he moves even closer to nuzzle my cheek with his own, the world spins away until it's just the two of us.

"Hey, Gabe," Tyler interrupts, breaking the moment.

I try to contain my frustration and blow a piece of hair out of my face. Gabe's fingers tense against my cheek, and if I weren't so close, I would have missed his low growl.

"What is it?" he asks.

Tyler's knowing smile splits his face. "Gotta couple questions for you. Paperwork."

Gabe's fingers knot in my hair. I burst out laughing. Tyler chuckles along with me.

"Swear to God, man, if you don't disappear, I'm banning you from the shack."

The smile fades from Tyler's lips. "That's low," he says.

"So is interrupting me when I'm in the middle of something. Again."

Tyler ignores Gabe's fierce scowl and holds up a hand to me. "Nice to see you again, Chloe," he says.

I take his hand and shake. "You, too."

"Five seconds," is all Gabe says.

Tyler laughs. "Good luck with this jackass. He's a handful."

Glancing back at the jackass in question, I just smile. "I think I can handle him."

He claps a hand on Gabe's back. "Make sure to drop by the station when you're feeling up to it."

Gabe jerks his chin in acknowledgment.

When we're alone again, he runs his hand over my hair.

"Look, I'm exhausted, you're exhausted. I've never been good at the emotional crap. The only thing I know is I don't want you to leave yet. I'd like to get to know you more, spend some time with you when we aren't getting shot at."

My smile builds slowly. "Boring, you mean."

"I could use a little boring," he says.

"Are you sure you aren't going to get tired of it after a while?"

He kisses me again, this time it's all languid strokes and softness. When he pulls away, he's breathing hard and he's anchored to me as much as I am to him. "Look, I can't see the future. Just...stay. Stay with me."

My heart swells at his request. I'm momentarily rendered speechless, so I do the only thing I can think of which doesn't need words. I lean toward him, a smile sitting on my lips, and kiss him.

GABRIEL

WEEKENDS USED to be my favorite time. I liked to spend them with Emily, teaching her how to fish on her Grandpa's old boat with Rudy happily scaring all of the fish in the near vicinity away, taking her to the beach to build sand castles taller than she was, or sleeping in and vegging on the couch with cartoons.

I don't know if I'm getting older, or the clocks in my house have all spontaneously sped up, but it seems as though the weekends grow shorter and shorter as time passes. This one felt like I blinked and it was gone.

Light filters through the window and spills across the beautiful woman sprawled naked on the bed next to me. It feels like she just got here and now it's already Sunday and time for her to go.

For the past year, Chloe had seamlessly become a part of

my weekend routine with Emily—who couldn't have been more overjoyed. If you asked her, she was ecstatic about having another girl in the house to recruit in her campaigns against me. I almost think Chloe comes each weekend to spend time with Emily as much as with me.

I can't find it in my heart to be jealous. I suppose it's my lot in life to be surrounded by beautiful women.

My alarm starts to blare, but I silence it with a swipe of my finger. Chloe stirs, but doesn't wake, and I spend the next half hour tracing her beautiful tanned skin with the backs of my fingers and the lightest pressure from my nails.

After a while, when her skin is covered in goose bumps, she comes awake with a languorous stretch. She blinks sleepily up at me and smiles. My fingers still in their quest across her skin and I zero in on her mouth.

"What is it?" she says and covers her lips with a hand as she yawns. I put a hand to her hip and pull her close. She squeals and pulls away, leaping from the bed still naked to back away from me. "Not before I brush my teeth!"

I smile and feel quite pleased with myself as she stalks across the room. Because in her hurry, she forgot to put clothes on, leaving all of my favorite parts visible. Water splashes in the bathroom and she hums. If that didn't cement my decision, I don't know what the hell would.

She comes out, still gloriously naked, and rests one hip on the edge of the bed. I frown at the distance between us and jerk her back with one smooth flex of my arm. She squawks and then her body is pressed against mine.

"What's gotten into you?" she asks, her voice muffled by a swift exhalation as I nip her throat.

"Let's stay in bed for a while," I say against her skin.

At my words, she softens beneath me, her arms coming around my waist, one staying on my back to soothe and the other diving into my hair. Her legs tangle with mine and she sighs contentedly in my ear.

"I really should go. I'll be back next weekend. I'm even going to see if I can get Friday off. Sienna still feels guilty even though it's been over a year. I can talk her into pretty much anything these days since I've mostly taken over the business."

"Yeah, I don't think that's going to work for me," I say as I wedge myself between her sweet thighs. Her legs go around my waist almost automatically, her feet digging into the backs of my legs. Color paints her cheeks a bright pink. I lean forward to kiss both of them in turn and then follow the flush down her neck to her chest. Her breathing grows more labored, then she gasps and grabs my hair with both hands just when things are getting interesting.

I frown up at her. "What?"

"What do you mean that's not going to work for you?" she asks.

Hitching my hips up, teasing her, I smirk when her hands ball into fists against me. "What do you think I mean?"

She can't talk for a second, and even when she does her voice is hoarse. "Don't, Gabe, it's too early. I need coffee before we start arguing."

"I've got what you need," I say, before I take one flushed nipple in my mouth.

I never get tired of her body, the way she responds to me. When I line myself up to her entrance and drive in with one thrust, her eyes widen and her mouth parts on a soundless scream. Her hands grapple for a hold on my shoulders, but I don't give her a second to adjust.

It takes me a few seconds to work through the searing pleasure that she isn't trying to hold onto me—she's hitting me.

I pause my thrusts, my cock swelling as I take in the flushing, seething mad female writhing beneath me. "What the hell are you doing?"

"How dare you?"

I catch her wrists in one hand and hold them above her head, far away from my vulnerable parts. Her hips jerk against me, but I've got her pinned to the bed so her movements only serve to drive us both completely insane.

"How dare I what?" I ask, my voice husky.

"You're breaking up with me during sex?" she asks incredulously.

"What the hell are you talking about?"

She gestures wildly with her head and rolls her eyes. "*This* isn't going to work for you?"

Words fail me, so I laugh against her throat.

"Oh, I'm glad you think this is so funny," she says.

I leverage up on one hand so I can use the other to brush away the hair from her face. Her eyes are glittering and her full lips are pressed into a line.

Using my thumb, I draw across her lower lip and then take it into my mouth, leaving it glistening from my attention. "I'm not breaking up with you, baby."

I take my finger now and swipe it across her lip to gather the moisture, then I trail it down her stomach. Her breath hitches in her chest when my hand reaches between us to stroke her.

"T-then what did you mean?"

"I want you," I say.

Her lips twitch. "Yeah, I think I got the message."

"No," I say, trying to concentrate on the right words, which is hard when she clenches around me like she's trying to make us two parts of one whole. "I mean I don't want you to leave."

Her expression softens and she leans up to kiss me with pouty lips. "I don't want to leave, either."

My pace quickens and her breath catches. "Then don't."

She arches, baring her neck to me and I lave kisses along the line of her throat. "God, if you don't get to the point, I'm going to go crazy here."

I take her face in my hands and capture her gaze with mine as she wraps her now free arms around me. We're connected in every possible way, and I wouldn't want it any other way.

"Marry me," I say.

"What?" she asks.

"Marry me," I say again.

"Oh, God, Gabe," she moans.

Her fingers dig into my sides and she constricts around me without warning. Throaty moans fill the air around me and I lose focus as everything goes white-hot.

A few minutes—or hours—later, when I manage to catch my breath, I say, "I'm going to take that as a yes."

Continue the *First to Fight Series* with...
WARRIOR!

ACKNOWLEDGMENTS

To Alana Albertson, Mia Searles, Elle Vanzandt and Ella Stewart. You have no idea how much your continued support has meant to me.

To my Knockouts! For all of your patience and enthusiasm.

I couldn't have submitted *Anchor* without the encouragement and love from my beta readers. YOU ROCK! This one's for you!

And finally to my daughter Afton. I hope all of your dreams come true.

 **Nicole Blanchard** is the *New York Times* and *USA Today* bestselling author of gritty romantic suspense and heartwarming new adult romance. She and her family reside in the south along with menagerie of animals. Visit her website www.authornicoleblanchard.com for more information or to subscribe to her newsletter for updates on sales and new releases.

facebook.com/authornicoleblanchard

twitter.com/blanchardbooks

instagram.com/authornicoleblanchard

amazon.com/Nicole-Blanchard

bookbub.com/authors/nicole-blanchard

goodreads.com/nicole_blanchard

pinterest.com/blanchardbooks

Dark Romance

Fantasy Romance

Standalone Novellas

Made in the USA
Middletown, DE
08 June 2021

41487400R00137